The
Nomad Harp

The
Nomad Harp

Laura
Matthews

Five Star • Waterville, Maine

Library of Congress Cataloging-in-Publication Data

Matthews, Laura.
   The nomad harp / Laura Matthews.
     p. cm.
   ISBN 0-7862-4529-8 (hc : alk. paper)
   I. Title.
   PS3563.A852 N66 2002
   813'.54—dc21   2002026775

For Paul, with Love

ONE

"It is out of the question, my dear aunt," he said firmly. "I am promised to Miss Forbes and there is no honorable way in which I can break that engagement."

"Fiddlesticks!" she returned, her cold black eyes raking his face. "A young lady of five and twenty will hardly be willing to wait a year to wed. She's on the shelf now, my boy, and you can be sure she has no intention of waiting a twelve-month with all its inherent hazards now that you are Viscount Pontley."

"I should think it all the more reason she would be willing to wait," he murmured.

"For your title? There's little enough in it, Pontley. My sons, God rest their souls, had no idea of estate management and were both addicted to gambling." There was no trace of grief in her hard, bitter face, though her body was encased in the deepest black bombazine of mourning and the room about them was shuttered and the furniture draped with black. "In your position it will be necessary for you to marry an heiress in order to restore Lockwood to its proper glory. Miss Forbes cannot bring you above two thousand pounds."

"Not so much, I assure you." The young man opposite her rose and paced about the room, his limp obvious to the old woman but ignored by himself. The years of naval activity brought a stiffness to his bearing which immediately identified him as a military man, and lent dignity to his height. His aunt studied the frowning face with its high forehead, intense

7

brown eyes and pursed lips. She was pleased with the progress her attack was making, but no indication of this appeared in her demeanor.

"Miss Forbes will realize that your change in position must allow for some leeway in the usual conventions. With a peerage you can look far above her for a bride, and in your year of mourning you are bound to be the object of a good deal of interest. She will only be distressed to see the caps flung at you by young ladies of unimpeachable birth."

"There is nothing wrong with her birth," he retorted with a scowl.

"Surely you must know that there is a question of her paternity!" his aunt exclaimed.

Pontley turned to regard her unbelievingly, "I know no such thing."

The Dowager Lady Pontley shook her head wonderingly. "Had you spent more time in London, you could not have missed hearing the rumors."

"I am not interested in gossip."

"When it concerns your prospective bride, you should be," she snapped.

"Mr. Forbes accepts her as his daughter. They are very devoted to one another."

"Indeed. I dare say she is the comfort of his old age, but there was a time when—"

"I will hear no more on the subject." Pontley's eyes blazed with annoyance and his chin, with its remarkable cleft, was set firmly.

"As you wish. No doubt your loyalty does you credit," she retorted sarcastically. "But it can only place Miss Forbes in an unenviable position to be brought into the light of public notice by marrying you. She had agreed to you as a husband when you were an unknown naval captain."

"Miss Forbes is familiar with London society, and is in regular correspondence with Lady Garth. I have never witnessed the least discomfort in her with regard to her birth. When she spent a season in London she was invited to all the best homes."

"No doubt she told you so herself." When the viscount did not respond to her jibe she continued, "Oh, I don't doubt Lady Garth writes to her, or even that Miss Forbes was indeed welcomed into a certain element of society. For a while there was a fascination with her playing of the harp, as I recall. But that was years ago, my dear nephew, and I have not been advised by any of my correspondents that Miss Forbes has endeavored to venture into society since that first season when her aunt brought her out. Do you not find that circumstance in itself suspicious?"

Pontley gave an exasperated shrug. "Why should I? I am not interested in attaining a position in society, nor ever have been. My means would have precluded it in any case, and it was hardly my object in offering for Miss Forbes."

"Why did you offer for her? I am told that she has no great beauty, no fortune, no talent in fact in any way except on the harp. Surely such a mouse could not have engaged your affections."

"Your opinion of Miss Forbes is irrelevant, Aunt, and I have no desire to discuss with you my reasons for offering for her."

Lady Pontley was not moved by this cut; her sensibilities were nonexistent and her feeling toward her nephew would have been one of contempt had he not now succeeded to the viscountcy. Within the span of a few weeks she had learned of the death of her younger son in India, and had witnessed the death of her elder son of the influenza which raged about the countryside. The news of Keith's death had taken months to reach them, along with the word that Lord Wellesley had taken Delhi, and when it arrived it came on top of the recent death of his older brother William, Viscount Pontley, stricken down by influenza, his body already ravaged by drink and excess. Lady Pontley herself proclaimed that it was the chill brought on by his exercises in the rain with the volunteers he commanded that had been his downfall, and no one questioned her. The habit of years was strong, and she showed every intention of attempting to direct her nephew's life as she had her sons', with as little success.

When she spoke, it was with biting sarcasm. "You have been elevated by your cousins' untimely deaths to a position of which you are not deserving, and it does not surprise me that you are willing to elevate a nobody with you. My sons had a proper regard for the consequence of their situation which you will never achieve, I fear. You have no regard for the respect due the Hobart name, young man, and turn a deaf ear to the advice of those older and wiser than yourself."

"Your interest in me is flattering, Aunt Gertrude, and I will overlook your rudeness in face of your double bereavement." He leaned against the mantelpiece to still the pain in his left leg. "I will respect your wishes insofar as waiting a year to wed is concerned, to show due deference to my cousins. It will mean a postponement of the wedding only, however, as I have no intention of breaking my promise to Miss Forbes. If she should have a desire to terminate our engagement in those circumstances, then your fondest wish will be granted. For my part, I cannot see that she would have any wish to do so, since it would be a more advantageous marriage than I was able to propose previously. Your visions of affluent young ladies tossing their caps at me are, if you will forgive me, ludicrous. If the position at Lockwood and the other estates is as bad as you imagine it, I am no prize in anything save

10

title, and my previous engagement will forestall even the heartiest of mamas from pushing their daughters forward, I should hope. I pray you will reconcile yourself to Miss Forbes and cause no dissension when we are wed."

"You are foolish beyond bearing, Pontley. Before you throw away your life I would advise you look into the circumstance of Lady Garth's friendship with your betrothed." When he made a gesture of dismissal she adopted a self-righteous pose. "I will say no more on the subject, you may be sure. It would behoove you to visit the estates in Gloucester and Somerset to bring them to some semblance of order after you have looked to Lockwood itself. You will find more than enough to keep you occupied for some time, I assure you. When you visit Huntley you must pay your respects to my brother's children near Tetbury. His older daughter, now Lady Morris, has her sister living with her. You will find the girl charming, accomplished and strikingly attractive, in addition to being an heiress. Your Miss Forbes could not hold a candle to her for birth or fortune."

"I shall be enchanted to make the acquaintance of your nieces," he retorted ironically. "My first destination must be Hastings, however, to speak with Miss Forbes. I shall convey your regards, as it would be most unwise for you to be at outs with her if she is so lacking in sensitivity as to maintain our betrothal."

"Your sarcasm is lost on me, Pontley. You are a babe in the wood when it comes to worldly knowledge and you will live to regret such an injudicious choice. What influence can she offer you? My niece at least has good political ties through her family, and mark my words, Pitt will resume the leadership of his party within the month. Addington is finished." The dowager waved a deprecating hand. "But then you are probably too innocent to know the value of such ties, though your naval career should have made you aware of them. Lady Garth is a follower of Fox," the old woman snorted, "and I have no doubt your Miss Forbes is as well."

"It is a matter of no concern to me."

"Fool! You are not in such a position that you can whistle down the wind some influence in Parliament. Do you think the fate of the Hobart estates rests only on their management? There are enclosures going forward near all of them. Your service in the navy will buy you no influence, my boy."

Pontley had only a vague understanding of the country-side. Left to his own resources at a young age, he had opted for the life at sea and had distinguished himself in the naval service. An authority on blockading and sprung masts, he had never had reason or desire to understand the functioning of an estate. His life had been devoted to his duties on board ship, which he had accomplished with ease and authority; to handling the crises of gales from the west which split masts and tore sails to tatters; to struggles with tides and rocks, which could be more hazardous than a weekly battle. He had suffered the seclusion from the world for months at a time which was the fate of sailors during the blockade of Brest. Only too aware of his ignorance of estate management, he had never expected nor even wished for his elevation to the viscountcy. In spite of the bland exterior he presented to his aunt, he was not unaware that her knowledge on the subject exceeded his by leaps and bounds.

"I don't doubt the truth of what you say, my dear aunt. It will take time for me to grasp the reins of the estates in my hands and obtain a satisfactory understanding of their working. Nonetheless, I am committed to Miss Forbes and no enticement of influence, wealth or birth can induce me to break my word to her. Let us speak no more of the matter. By your leave, I would appreciate an early evening so that I may start for Hastings in the morning."

"It is your house now," she replied bitterly, "and you may retire and rise at your own leisure. I will be removing to the dower house within the month."

"I pray you will not move with undue haste, Aunt Gertrude. There is not the slightest need for your removal at such a distressing time for you, and I have no idea when I will take up residence here."

His aunt scowled on him. "I have no desire to remain where I am not wanted and where my advice is held in low regard."

"I assure you I am not unaware of your greater understanding of the estate than my own, and I shall not be impervious to your advice on such matters, Aunt. On other matters I must be guided by my own principles. You will need several months, I should imagine, to recover from your recent shock and to plan the removal of your belongings to the dower house." He watched the old tartar's lips twitch with triumph.

"That is kind of you, nephew. I shall look about for a companion to assist me in my move, as I have not the strength at this time to carry out the necessary tasks."

Pontley pitied the companion her lot, but said nothing further on the matter. He retreated to his room not entirely easy in his mind, in spite of his proclamation to his aunt. The problem was that he did not really know Miss Forbes all that well owing to his life at sea. After hours, days, months, of loneliness on board ship he had been intrigued on meeting her by her vivacity and her calm capability. But most of all he had been won over when he heard her play the harp, as many others were. Her skill was extraordinary and he had envisioned quiet evenings by the fireside listening to her play. True, she was not a beauty, but she was well enough to look at, and with an ease of making friends which he could not but admire. His own years away from the ordinary intercourse of society had made him uncomfortable amongst the gently bred until he had met her and been accepted into her own circle of acquaintance. Not that he was not well liked by the officers and men whom he met in his naval duties; with them there was no question of being ill at ease. Their life was his and he partook of it freely and with enthusiasm. He had not intended to change his way of life, and had been forced to only by the dual necessity of his injury and his accession to the viscountcy.

His aunt had impressed upon him the necessity of undertaking the management of the estates, with their hundreds of families dependent upon the lord of the manor for their livelihood and well-being. Still, he knew nothing of such matters and would have retreated to the sea had it not been for his injury. It was a time when every knowledgeable sailor and naval officer was needed to prevent invasion by the French flotilla, but the wound did not heal properly, continued to cause pain, and he might be left with a perpetual limp. He wondered what Miss Forbes would think of that.

Surprising that she had accepted him, when he came to think of it. The life he had offered her was one of continual absence, of meager means and no social position beyond his connection with the Hobarts at Lockwood, who completely ignored him. The reverse was likely to be true now, aside from the precarious financial position his cousin William had left. Would the transition from Captain Philip Hobart to Viscount Pontley indeed impress Miss Forbes? Why had she chosen to accept him when there were half a dozen men in her circle only too ready to carry her off as a bride? That was unusual enough in itself, considering her age and lack of fortune, but he knew for a fact that it was true. Had he not spoken with two of her rejected suitors before he, at twenty-eight years of age, had put his own case to the test?

Under his aunt's attack, he had had little to say except that he did not intend to undertake the dishonorable course of breaking off his engagement. Her insinuations had left him nonplussed, and annoyed with his lack of knowledge of his prospective bride. He drew a hand wearily through his crop of straight brown hair. Everything had seemed so simple at the time. They would marry—a comfortable sort of arrangement whereby he would have someone to come home to from his duties at sea. She would bear him children and raise them, and he would spoil them when he was on leave. He had in fact been in the process of negotiating for a house in Hastings when his aunt had summoned him to Lockwood with the news that his cousin William was dead. Only a week after his arrival, the news of Keith's death reached them, and his aunt had been seized with a frenzy such as he had never before seen. Her grief was not so much for the loss of her sons, but for the loss of the Pontley title to him, an outsider.

Under her storm of invective he had attempted to calm her agitation, and in time she had shifted the balance of rage to a premeditated assault on his choice of a bride. With deadly calm now she proceeded to undermine his purpose and propose her own niece as a far more fitting viscountess. Pontley could see that the thought of her niece in such a situation was a salve to her wounded sense of what was proper. And he could see that she hoped through her niece to maintain some of her fast-diminishing power. What he could not see was whether her intimations had any basis in fact and whether they would affect him if he married Miss Forbes. It seemed unlikely that she would pass on groundless rumors to him, knowing that sooner or later he would find out the truth of the matter. She had never met Miss Forbes, however, and information she had was doubtless on hearsay from old crones with whom she corresponded.

15

Nonetheless, the calm, uncomplicated life he had envisioned had been ruthlessly shattered during the past month and he saw no hopes of piecing it together with any semblance of pleasure to him. Would the Miss Forbes he had envisioned as his comfort on leave prove a satisfactory companion in the continuous setting of lady of the manor?

TWO

Glenna Forbes was not even aware of the possibility of becoming a viscountess. Her last communication from Captain Philip Hobart had been a hurried note informing her that his cousin William had died and that he was setting out for the Lockwood estate. Aware that he was possessed of two cousins, though she knew little more of his family, she naturally assumed that the younger had assumed the peerage. Her own father had suffered from the influenza which had carried off Captain Hobart's cousin, and her days were spent nursing him. With his gradual recovery she once again took up the threads of her life, surprised at not having word from Captain Hobart but not alarmed, considering the circumstance which had drawn him to Lockwood.

It was therefore most unexpected when a Viscount Pontley was announced to her as she sat in the morning room playing the harp. Puzzled, she agreed to receive the visitor, since he must certainly be her betrothed's cousin. Her confusion made her miss the twinkle in the butler's eye, and she stared at Pontley for some time when he entered, unable to decide how to greet him. When the door was closed behind him and he approached her, she became aware of his limp.

"You have hurt yourself."

"Not much, I assure you, though it is possible I shall retain the limp." Her concern appeared genuine and Pontley took her hand and pressed it. "I have not seen you since my ship was engaged in a slight skirmish and I carelessly stood in the way of a ball. It has been removed, but the wound heals too slowly."

Glenna nodded and, taking a seat, motioned him to do likewise. Indicating his civilian dress she asked, "Have you resigned your commission in the Navy?"

"I have succeeded to my cousin's title, Miss Forbes, and have responsibilities in that direction now."

"I see. I thought you had two cousins, Cap—Lord Pontley."

The interview was not proceeding as he had expected and he replied stiffly, "While at Lockwood we received word that my cousin Keith who was serving in India under Lord Wellesley had been killed in the autumn."

"Your poor aunt! How could she bear to lose two sons in so short a space of time? I offer you both my condolences." Her blue eyes were troubled and the fair, smooth skin wrinkled into a frown. "Should you not have stayed with your aunt?"

"My presence only adds to her grief."

Glenna was startled by his obvious lack of sympathy and found herself unable to reply. Under his scrutiny she felt uncomfortable, and rose to ring for refreshments. He politely rose with her and watched her cross to the pull. There was the same calm efficiency of movement he had noted and approved on previous visits. The blue muslin gown was becoming and modest, the white cap delightfully fantastic, almost as though it were a laughing reminder of her age. But where he was used to seeing the blue eyes lively with enthusiasm, now they were downcast and troubled. The reddish-blond hair curled about her face in a frame, and the nose was rather short and turned up perhaps too much for real beauty, but he thought once again that she was an attractive woman. And she had nothing to say to him. When she turned to find him studying her she made a small gesture of helplessness with her hands and remained silent.

"You have not congratulated me on my new title, Miss Forbes."

"In the circumstances I find it difficult. It necessitated the deaths of two of your cousins, which must have caused your aunt untold grief, and I see no sign of sorrow in you." She remained standing with her back against the wall, feeling almost at bay.

"I am not in the habit of exhibiting my emotions, Miss Forbes, and I had little acquaintance with my cousins. Nonetheless, I have agreed to my aunt's wish that I postpone my marriage for a year in suitable mourning for them."

"I commend you on the propriety of your decision, Lord Pontley, and appreciate that you had no time to consult me on such a matter. I shall call a halt to the preparations that are in progress, of course." She turned to give instructions to the footman who had entered and then resumed her seat. "I cannot feel so sanguine, however, on your decision to abandon your career."

"I cannot very well manage the running of three estates if I am at sea, Miss Forbes, to say nothing of the incapacity caused by my wound." He unconsciously tapped this injured member with an angry finger. "My cousin has left his affairs in a sad state, I fear, which will require a great deal of my time to straighten out."

"To say nothing of your lack of knowledge on the subject," she murmured.

"What would you have me do, Miss Forbes? Leave matters to sort themselves out? Return to my ship and turn my back on those dependent on the estates?"

"Your decision may very well be the right one, sir, but I cannot feel that you will be comfortable being a country squire after your years at sea."

"I shall hate it, Miss Forbes. And you? Does it make a difference to you?" His intent brown eyes held hers forcefully.

"Yes, it makes a vast difference to me, Lord Pontley. Not the life so much, you understand, but that you did not feel it necessary to speak with me before taking your decision."

His eyes opened incredulously. "You are annoyed that I did not consult you, Miss Forbes, and perhaps allow you to make the decision?"

Glenna bit her lip to force back the retort she wished to make. How had she ever become engaged to this man? How could she have overlooked his insensitivity and autocratic manner? It did occur to her to wonder if she was refining too much on the matter, and she sat silent considering the possibility.

"You do not answer me, ma'am. Are you vexed that you did not have the opportunity to sway my mind? Had you rather have a husband who is away at sea the better part of the year?"

"Yes," she flashed at him, "that is precisely what I wish." Although it was not altogether true, there was enough truth in it to pique her.

Pontley rose abruptly and winced at the pain his swift movement caused him. With an elaborate bow, he muttered, "You must pardon me, ma'am. Had I known, of course I would have rejected the viscountcy and retained my position in the Royal Navy. There are some ladies, I believe, who would be delighted to find themselves engaged to a peer when all they had hoped for was a mere sailor. I see you are not one of them, though, and I offer you my most humble apology." His burning eyes belied any humility; he stood poker straight, every fiber of his being awash with anger.

"Oh, pray sit down, for God's sake, and let us discuss the

matter rationally." When he continued to tower over her, glaring all the more, she rubbed her eyes distractedly and attempted to calm herself. After a moment she said gently, "I did not mean to upset you, sir, by intimating that I wished to be rid of you when we were married, or by seeming to wish to order you about. I will grant that I am given to a certain measure of independence which is not perhaps acceptable to you in one of my sex." She raised her eyes to meet his, and found them unyielding. "Would you like me to cry off?"

Stunned, he could not bring himself to speak. There was nothing he wished more at the moment, but it seemed wrong to him that she should suggest such a thing after attempting, however unsuccessfully, to apologize. He sat down.

Glenna smiled her appreciation of this move. "Perhaps I should tell you why I accepted your offer, Lord Pontley, so that you can understand my situation. My father's health is indifferent and he lives in perpetual fear of dying and leaving me unprovided for. I cannot like the additional strain this worry puts on him and I had determined to marry to ease his mind. Not that I have anything against marriage in itself, you understand, but I am aware that my years of freedom have engendered in me an independence which does not perhaps bode well for marriage. Therefore it seemed wise to choose a man who . . . would not be continually harassed by my independence, and who would not be always about to keep too firm a hand on the reins, so to speak."

Although his face had become a blank, Glenna saw the muscle at the corner of his mouth twitch. "I know several men who would not keep any rein on me at all, of course, but I would be just as unsatisfied with such an arrangement as with too heavy a hand. It seemed to me that you answered my situation very well. When you were on leave you could be in charge of the household, but for the most part you would be away and I would be free to run my own life as I saw fit."

"You make it sound very practical."

"I assure you it was. Do not think that I would not have done everything in my power to provide you with a comfortable home, for it seemed to me that that was precisely what you required. I know you are fond of the harp and are satisfied to be accepted into the circles in which I move, without making an effort to develop social contacts of your own. So you see, when you came here today in a rather belligerent frame of mind, and informed me that everything had changed. . . ."

"I was not aware that I came to you in a belligerent frame of mind."

"I may be mistaken about that, I grant you, though I cannot help but feel you were ill at ease to present me with your news. The impression you conveyed to me was that I could accept these changes willy-nilly or break the engagement, and that you would as soon have the latter as the former."

"The necessity of a year's wait did strike me as a possible point of annoyance to you, Miss Forbes."

"It is, Lord Pontley, but I can accept the inevitability. My father would be happy to see me settled sooner, but for myself I cannot mind."

"Another year of freedom for you," he murmured.

"You might look at it that way," she admitted with a grin which lit the blue eyes. "Now that you understand my situation a little better, I shall ask you again: would you like me to cry off?"

He regarded her ruefully. "How am I to answer such a question? It is apparent that you have grave doubts as to whether we could live together comfortably under the changed conditions, but on the other hand your father will have the same worry on his hands if you do not marry. From my small acquaintance with your circle of young people, I would say you have already rejected every eligible male you know."

Her eyes danced appreciatively. "That does not preclude my meeting someone new."

"To be sure," he said curtly, "but your age is a disadvantage."

"Do not let that hamper you in your decision, Lord Pontley. I do not."

"It is not my decision. I stand by my offer for you. If you are willing to accept the change, then we will be married in a year." His leg had begun to ache and he shifted uncomfortably in his chair.

"In that case I should like a month or two to make a decision. Perhaps during that time I could meet your aunt and see Lockwood, and we would have a chance to get to know one another better."

"I fear my aunt would not welcome a visit from you at just this time," he said stiffly, "and it will be necessary for me to spend the next few months visiting the estates in Gloucestershire and Somerset."

"Very well. We will terminate the engagement now, then, and I thank you for your kindness in offering for me, Lord Pontley." She rose and offered him her hand, her frank eyes never leaving his face.

"You misunderstand, Miss Forbes," he protested, wincing as he rose rapidly to his feet. "I did not mean to put obstacles in the way of your suggestion, but my aunt will be looking for a companion preparatory to moving to the dower house and will be much occupied. She has convinced me of the necessity of seeing to the other estates, as they are in desperate need of some management. There is no need to make a hasty decision. I will call on you on my return for your answer."

Glenna sighed and nodded her head. "As you wish. A few months can make no difference to either of us at this point."

THREE

With the recovery of Mr. Forbes's health in mind, Glenna informed him only that her betrothed had sustained a great change in his circumstances. He was delighted with the news that his daughter would be marrying into the peerage and have a country estate on which to live, but he was not wholly oblivious to her dispassionate rehearsal of this information. The thought did occur to him that she was not entirely pleased with the new arrangement.

"You must not mind that you will be living away from Hastings," he comforted her. "I shall go on here very well."

She forced a laugh. "I place great reliance on Mrs. Booth, Papa." The housekeeper was indeed loyal to her employer, and Glenna trusted that she would be called in any emergency. "Besides, we must wait a year to marry, so I shall not have to face such a parting for some time. Perhaps Lord Pontley will allow me to have you at Lockwood for a period each year. There was so much to discuss that I had no time to ask him."

"A short visit now and then to see how you go on would indeed be welcome," he admitted with a tender smile, "but I would not have you press him to keep me there for a protracted stay. I am fond of my house, and Hastings, and I have my work here. You will wish to have time alone with your husband."

Glenna murmured an affirmative reply and, feeling guilty for her deception, offered to play for him. As the days passed she grew more upset by Pontley's lack of sympathy for his aunt's plight, and she evolved a plan by which she might help soften the old woman's sufferings. Lockwood was located not far from Haywards Heath, and Glenna had a cherished friend who lived with her parents at the vicarage in Burgess Hill. It would require a certain amount of deception in itself, but Glenna could excuse that on the basis of the good she would be doing, since her erstwhile fiancé obviously intended no assistance whatever to his bereaved aunt.

Phoebe Thomas was delighted to receive her friend's letter, but it puzzled her that Glenna should be asking the vicar for a letter of recommendation for her cousin, and especially that such a letter should be sent to the Dowager Lady Pontley. True, the vicar knew Glenna's cousin Mary Stokes, but it was inconceivable to Phoebe that Mary, who was placid to the point of indolence, could desire a post as companion to the dowager. It was even more suspicious that any reply to this offer was to be sent to Glenna herself, since Phoebe had but the day before received a letter, perhaps rather one would call it a note, from Mary herself saying that she was bound to London for the season. Since Phoebe was not unfamiliar with Glenna's youthful pranks, she had some misgivings, but she nevertheless caused the vicar to dispatch such a letter to the dowager and within a matter of days received a reply which she dutifully forwarded to Glenna.

It seemed to Glenna that it could make no difference whatever to the dowager who she took for a companion, provided the companion served her well. If Pontley thought it would upset his aunt to meet Glenna at such a time (and she could understand that the bereaved woman might be distressed to have her successor as mistress at Lockwood to stay just now), then she should meet someone else who would offer her the comfort and assistance she must need at such a time. There was, of course, the possibility that the deception would have to be revealed later if Glenna did indeed marry Pontley, but she considered this highly unlikely. For the present she wished only to provide some comfort to the distressed woman, since Pontley apparently felt no obligation to do so.

The reply from the dowager was short and to the point. She stated her requirements, the wages she was prepared to pay, and wrote that if the terms were agreeable to Mary Stokes, she was to present herself at Lockwood one week from the day of writing to be employed on a probationary basis. Glenna, while making allowances for the dowager's emotional state, still had a qualm when she read the letter. The imperious tone and niggardly wage offered did not suggest a personality with which she was likely to live in harmony. That could not be helped, however, and she felt herself committed to provide what solace she could, so she advised her father that she would be heading for Phoebe Thomas's for a period of time. Mr. Forbes, his health recovered, was delighted that his daughter should be released from her nursing duties and have the opportunity to go visiting for a while. He agreed to direct his letters to Phoebe, as Glenna remarked that she would be staying at other places as well, but would always contact Phoebe for her correspondence.

When all was in readiness and the post chaise ordered, Mr. Forbes frowned at the portmanteaux in the hall and turned to his daughter. "Do you not intend to take your harp, Glenna? The vicar has remarked more than once on how much pleasure it gives him to hear you play."

In her nervousness about the whole venture, Glenna very nearly betrayed herself. Her second thoughts suddenly seemed very rational and she was disposed to give up the whole project. Why should not Pontley take care of his own aunt? But her heart cried out for the deserted dowager and she calmly replied, "I fear the harp will take up too much space, Papa."

"Oh, no, my dear, it will be worth the inconvenience, and will in some measure repay the vicar for his kindness in having you. I will direct that it be brought down."

Glenna nodded acquiescence and wondered desperately how the vicar would feel about having a harp left in his small home while she went elsewhere, for she had no intention of descending on Lockwood with it. Companions did not travel about with harps, no matter how gently born they were. With a shrug of resignation she watched the awkward instrument bundled into the post chaise, where it barely left room for her and the maid who was to accompany her to Burgess Hill. "I think May had best not come, Papa. I will be no more than four hours on the road and we could not but be cramped to death."

Her father reluctantly agreed when he surveyed the crowded interior. "Very well, Glenna. Perhaps I should not insist that you take the harp."

His worried expression brought forth a cheerful smile from his daughter. "Nonsense. I would miss playing, you know, and the vicar will be pleased. Perhaps Phoebe will take the opportunity to learn." She hoped fervently that her friend would do so; otherwise there was absolutely no purpose in bringing the instrument with her at all.

After a fond parting, Glenna disposed herself as comfortably as she was able and, despite the roughness of the passage, entered her thoughts in her journal as she progressed. Putting them down helped to solidify her purpose, and she arrived at the vicarage with more determination than she had left her home. She planned to spend one night with her friend before progressing to Lockwood, where instinct cautioned her she would need every ounce of her resources.

Phoebe stared in amazement at the harp when the steps were let down for her friend to descend. "Dear God, Glenna, I had no idea you meant to bring the harp for such a short stay."

"Never mind, love, I will explain." Glenna whispered this aside before turning to the vicar and his wife, who appeared no less astonished as the postillion struggled to release the instrument from where it had become securely lodged in the chaise. It took the combined efforts of the postillion and one of the Thomas's servants to unload the unwieldy harp and convey it into the vicarage.

The vicar and his wife politely refrained from commenting on the invasion of their diminutive home by the instrument, but Phoebe's eyes indicated her desire to get Glenna alone for the promised explanation. As soon as she could do so without appearing rude, Glenna excused herself from tea and asked Phoebe to escort her to her room.

When the door was closed behind them, Phoebe caught her hand and demanded, "What is going forward, Glenna? Are you up to some mischief?"

"I suppose you would say so, Phoebe, though I assure you it is with the best of intentions." Glenna's eyes danced with merriment. "I thought you might enjoy learning to play the harp."

"Pooh, you thought nothing of the kind, my dear friend. Do you intend to leave that . . . monster with us?" she asked incredulously.

"I'm afraid I shall have to, love. I cannot very well take it to Lockwood with me, now, can I?" Taking pity on her confused friend, Glenna proceeded to unfold the story of her engagement and her decision to befriend the dowager.

"Well, it is very kind of you, I suppose," Phoebe pronounced doubtfully, "but I do not think my father would like being a party to such a deception."

"Shall I tell him the whole, Phoebe? You see, I cannot think Pontley's aunt would be comfortable with me as myself, and yet I cannot believe that she is not in the most desperate need for consolation at such a time. Pontley has been most callous about the whole thing, and I really cannot think I will marry him in the end. If you think I should tell your papa, I will do so, and abandon the scheme."

Pheobe's brow wrinkled with concentration. "Well, he did no more than write a recommendation for your cousin, after all, and so long as he does not know what you plan, there can be no blame for him. I know he would approve of your kindness in the matter, Glenna, so perhaps we shall not bother him with the details." She smiled mischievously. "I have heard nothing to indicate that the dowager's temperament is conciliating, so you are apt to be only too well rewarded for your efforts."

"Even a disagreeable woman deserves comfort and assistance at such a time," Glenna retorted self-righteously.

And Glenna recognized immediately when she met the dowager that she was indeed a most disagreeable woman. Her attitude toward her new companion was condescending, and, meaning to start as she meant to go on, she immediately set Glenna about numerous tasks of an irritating and demeaning nature. She bullied and chided the young woman, and was immensely pleased when her new Mary accepted all this complacently.

Relegated to an attic room with a tiny, dirty window, Glenna promptly set about cleaning it, though she was twice interrupted in the small task by a summons from the dowager. When she finally had an opportunity to survey the view, she was delighted by the gently rolling hills with their coppices, the fields and the Home Farm. Used as she was to her daily sight of the channel in Hastings, the lake was a welcome vision, and she determined to explore the estate if she were ever given a moment's peace.

The dowager set her to listing the items of personal property which were to be conveyed to the dower house, and as the list grew daily, Glenna began to wonder if the old woman intended to leave Pontley any furniture at all. Occasionally Lady Pontley would make an aside which Glenna interpreted to mean that a specific item was not indeed her own but belonged with the estate, but since her nephew was unfamiliar with the place he would never know the difference. These semiconfidences embarrassed her and she strove to turn a deaf ear to them. Pontley would have to look after his own interests.

As the weeks passed and Glenna could see no sign in the dowager of any grief for her sons, she began to consider the possibility of leaving on some pretext. She did not mind the work she did, although the dowager, encouraged by her willingness, increased the load daily, but her purpose in coming seemed to have dissipated. Here was no heartbroken mother mourning her sons; rather the old woman bitterly denounced them as ungrateful and disobedient wretches. Lady Pontley reserved a special store of invective for her nephew, whom she apostrophized as a fool and an interloper. Glenna had very nearly decided to tell the old woman that her father had fallen ill and she must return home, when the dowager herself succumbed to a putrid sore throat which forced her to bed. From this position she continued to order Glenna about unceasingly, but a large share of the young lady's duties now became concerned with the estate. Glenna, fascinated to be able to learn something of the workings of the country, determined to continue on until her employer was again restored to health.

The day came when a letter from Pontley arrived for his aunt and Glenna found herself, on delivering it, instructed to break the seal and read it to her. She pleaded her lack of desire to do so on the basis that it might contain personal information.

"That is highly unlikely, Miss Stokes, as the chucklehead has little to say to me beyond upholding his honor in a misguided engagement."

Appalled by her position, Glenna thrust the letter into Lady Pontley's hands and turned to leave. "Stay and read me the letter!" the dowager rasped. "How dare you rush off that way? Sit down this minute."

Glenna mutely received the letter back and perched herself on the edge of an uncomfortable chair. She was too shaken to attempt to organize her thoughts as quickly as was her wont, so she obediently unfolded the sheet and began to read, "My dear aunt, I hope this note finds you well and in reasonable spirits. Since last I wrote I have been at Huntley attempting to sort out the management of the estate here. I have replaced the agent with a young man who seems capable as well as knowledgeable, as your son's agent struck me as neither. The methods used here have been in practice for hundreds of years, which may recommend them on antiquity but hardly on efficiency. Mr. Brown (the new agent) assures me that the acreage is good and can turn a profit if handled properly. He has been doing his best to interest me in turnips and wheat, but the learning process is slow. The freshly turned earth smells delightful and the budding plants are promises of a fruitful harvest just as important to the nation at such a time as our ships, I imagine, so I console myself."

Her reading was interrupted here by the old woman's snort of vexation. "He can never turn himself from a sailor into a farmer and would do better not to try. What a fool he sounds blathering of such things!"

Glenna's impression had been otherwise; she had been touched by Pontley's simple response to the land and his efforts to accommodate himself to a wholly unfamiliar way of life. The conclusion of the letter was to reverse their positions. "I have paid my respects to Lord and Lady Morris and Miss Jennifer Stafford at Cromer Lodge as you requested. Miss Stafford is indeed a most striking young lady, possessed of an elfin charm and winsomeness quite foreign to my experience—one moment dashing about the estate at breakneck speed on her white mare and the next seated next to one full of confidences, wit and an odd assortment of miscellaneous knowledge. I will grant you, my dear aunt, that she possesses those virtues of which you spoke, and she does not seem indifferent to me, but I am determined on that course to which I am in honor bound. I shall go to Manner Hall in Somerset soon, though I intend to stay here another week for the felicitous company. Your very obedient servant and nephew, Pontley."

Lady Pontley absolutely gloated over this conclusion, sure that Pontley would manage to extract himself from his engagement now. In spite of her obvious desire to share her triumph with her companion, Glenna excused herself as firmly as she had ever done with the old woman. In her room she meditated on the harvest she was reaping from her crop of deception, and upbraided herself for such a prank. Not only had Pontley proved correct in leaving his aunt to her own devices, but he was certainly in a position where he would prefer to have the engagement broken, and only maintained it out of a sense of obligation. Glenna sat down immediately and penned a letter to him assuring him that she was determined to terminate their engagement. She thanked him again for the honor he had done her and hoped that he would enjoy a prosperous and comfortable life at Lockwood.

There was nothing she wished more to do then than pack her portmanteaux and flee from the place, but on answering a summons from the dowager she found the old woman had suffered a relapse, quite probably brought on by her excess of joy, Glenna thought exasperatedly. She settled into her duties once again and nursed the old woman through her slow recovery.

FOUR

Pontley received his fiancée's letter the day before he intended leaving for Manner Hall. Since she had promised to wait until he came to her for her decision, he was surprised to receive so firm a rejection. It occurred to him that she might have met with an acceptable man to replace him, which, he thought ruefully, would not be so difficult to do given her requirements, and his current inability to fall in line with them. However likely that might be, the very decidedness of her letter produced a suspicion in him that there was something amiss. The more he considered the matter the more he determined that his aunt might have had a hand in this precipitate decision on Miss Forbes's part. He would not put it past the old harridan to write his fiancée in such terms as would make her write such a letter to him.

Instead of leaving for Manner Hall, he headed for Hastings, as Glenna had given him reason to believe that she would be there. Mr. Forbes welcomed him kindly, though he was uncertain as to how to treat the young man, for he, too, had received a letter from Glenna advising him that she had broken off the engagement. Since Mr. Forbes had developed a respect for the young man whom he had expected to be his future son-in-law, the news had come as an unwelcome shock to him. There were not many young men, in his opinion, who would be able to exercise the proper control over his strong-willed daughter, and Lord Pontley was the only one he had met.

"Is Miss Forbes away from home?" Pontley asked, when no effort was made to send for her.

"She has been visiting a friend at Burgess Hill for some time, though she travels about from there, and I can never be sure precisely where she is. I simply direct my letters to her there, and she is careless in hers as to where she is at any given time." He appeared perplexed by this aberration in his daughter and wished to make some excuse for her, but could think of none.

"I should like to speak with her. No doubt you have been informed that she has chosen to cry off."

"Yes," Mr. Forbes sighed. "I am sorry to hear it, my lord. I would like to see her comfortably settled, and I cannot doubt that she would be with you."

"Perhaps she has transferred her affections to another young man," Pontley suggested impassively.

Surprised, Mr. Forbes said stiffly, "There has been no suggestion of such a thing. I cannot recall her even mentioning a man in her letters. My daughter is not given to erratic behavior, and would hardly flit about in such a manner. She chose you after careful consideration, and after years of not lacking for suitors, I promise you. Your new situation can only enhance her position."

"She was not pleased with my new situation."

"Nonsense! How could she not be?"

"She had accepted for a husband a man who would be away at sea a good deal of the time, and found herself subsequently engaged to one who would be underfoot."

Mr. Forbes, at first wont to regard this as flippant, after a moment considered it seriously. "Did she tell you so?"

"Yes, though more politely."

"But she continued the engagement after you had been here to tell her of the change."

"It was a temporary arrangement; she desired time to think matters over."

"I see." Mr. Forbes determinedly considered the significance of his daughter's actions. At length he lifted tired gray eyes to the intent brown ones opposite him. "I am sure she meant you no harm, sir. If there is a culprit in the case it is myself with my fears of leaving her stranded. Do you mean to go to Burgess Hill to speak with her?"

"Yes."

"Then I pray you will tell her she is never to marry on my account alone. She is a clever girl and will be able to manage without a husband. I have always known that, of course, but marriage for her seemed a more suitable solution."

"I will tell her, sir." Pontley rose and offered his hand to the older man. "Your daughter assessed the situation accurately, and I don't doubt all would have been well enough had not both of my cousins died."

Mr. Forbes nodded his understanding. "Give her my love."

But Pontley was unable to give Glenna her father's love because of course he did not find her at the vicarage. When he was announced, Phoebe had the most horrid foreboding that the truth was about to come out and she tried desperately to prevent it. Pontley was at first puzzled, and then amused, by her machinations, which eventually led to her taking him on a tour of the vicarage gardens.

"Perhaps you would explain to me, Miss Thomas, why my presence so upsets you," he suggested with exaggerated politeness.

Phoebe bit her lip and contemplated an answer which would not altogether throw the fat into the fire. "Well, you see, my lord, my parents are not aware . . . that is, Glenna is not here and my parents have no idea where she is and do not expect her."

"And yet her harp is resting in your drawing room."

A flush followed by a giggle greeted this remark. "Yes, I have been attempting to learn how to play it."

"Where is Miss Forbes?"

"I should not like to say, my lord."

"Her father believes that she is here or visiting around the neighborhood."

"Yes."

"Yes, what? Is she visiting in the neighborhood?"

"Not precisely. She would not wish for you to know where she is, Lord Pontley, though I assure you she is perfectly safe and well."

He frowned. "Do you mean to tell me that she is somewhere her father would not approve, Miss Thomas?"

Phoebe bent to pick a flower and kept her eyes on the border. Evasively she replied, "I could reach her for him in the matter of an hour, had he need of her."

"That hardly answers my question, Miss Thomas."

"I think he would not *dis*approve, if he understood the whole story." Phoebe felt pinned by his eyes and squirmed uncomfortably. "There is no need to tell him, you know, for she will be home in just a short time now."

Pontley emitted an exasperated sigh. "Very well, Miss Thomas. I will disturb your peace no further, but if I find she is not in Hastings within the week I will be forced to inform her father of this . . . escapade."

"Thank you, sir. I will make sure that she is home by then."

"Please excuse me to your parents. I would find it difficult to face them again in the circumstances."

Phoebe watched him walk away with relief, and went in directly to write a note to Glenna. She dispatched it within the hour by a messenger who unfortunately dawdled on the way.

Glenna was having one of her rare breaks from the dowager, and even then she was performing a task for her. But she delighted in being in the sunlight with the smell of the warm strawberries all about her and the chance to slip a few in her mouth as she gathered them. It was rare for them to have a visitor at Lockwood and she squinted her eyes against the sun when she heard hoofbeats on the gravel drive. The visitor did not stop at the house but drove around to the stables and alighted there. Not until he began to walk toward the house, a progress which would take him right past her, did she recognize him; the limp betrayed his identity before ever she could see his face clearly.

For a moment she thought to dash away from him, but that would only draw his attention. Instead she continued to pick the strawberries as calmly as she could, gradually turning her back to him. If he would just go into the house she could slip in the back way and up to her room without being seen. Somehow she would manage to pack and be away from Lockwood before he could see her, and she would never be discovered because his aunt would only inform him that a Miss Stokes had most mysteriously and ungratefully disappeared.

Unfortunately, Pontley, having observed what the young woman was doing, conceived a strong desire to taste the strawberries. He strode over to her and remarked, "Quite a fine early crop. I had no idea there were strawberries." Her lack of response drew his second gaze, and for a moment he stood speechless. "What the *devil* are *you* doing here?!"

Glenna dropped a demure curtsy and murmured, "It's a long story, my lord."

"I have sufficient time to hear every word of it." He stood, hands on buckskin-clad hips, glowering down at her.

"Surely there is no hurry. You must wish to wash the dust from your face."

"And give you time to make your escape? You sadly underestimate me, my dear girl. I will hear your story right now."

"I feel so foolish," she whispered.

"You *look* foolish, Miss Forbes. What are you dressed up to be—the milkmaid?"

Glenna lifted her chin defiantly and plucked at the frumpy brown cotton gown. "I am dressed in accordance with my role as your aunt's companion, Lord Pontley."

"Did she require you to change the color of your hair?" he asked angrily.

"No, of course not. That was a touch of my own," she admitted proudly. "I thought if I powdered it I would look older."

"You look ridiculous, Miss Forbes." He grasped the modest cap which rested on her silvery curls and tossed it on the ground. "Shake it out."

"The powder will ruin my gown," she protested.

"Your gown should be burned in any case!"

"Do you want me to take if off, too?" she asked pertly.

"Shake the powder out of your hair, Miss Forbes."

Glenna obediently attempted to pat the powder from her springy curls. When she was only minimally successful, her ex-fiancé ruthlessly assisted her until the red-gold could once more be seen, and then he dusted the powder from her face with his handkerchief.

"Very well. I am ready to hear your story now."

"You have ruined the strawberries and gotten powder on your coat," she pointed out.

"Miss Forbes, my patience is running out. Begin."

She sighed forbearingly. "I thought you were very callous to leave your aunt here alone when she had just lost both of her sons, and you mentioned that she was looking for a companion."

"I also mentioned that she would not be interested in seeing you."

"Yes, and I thought it politic to come here as my cousin, Mary Stokes, who is in London and would not, I feel sure, mind my borrowing her name for a while."

"You arranged this, I presume, through your friend at the vicarage in Burgess Hill?"

"Have you gone and upset Phoebe? That is very unkind of you, my lord."

"How was I to know that my coming there to find you would upset her? She promised to have you back with your father in a week, but would not tell me where you were."

"She is very loyal. I wonder how she has progressed on the harp."

"Not well, I should imagine," he drawled. "I must ask you to return to the matter in hand, Miss Forbes."

"There is little more to tell. I did come to your aunt and she accepted me as her companion and I have been here ever since."

"Surely you must have realized the utter uselessness of your position."

"Well, I did, you know, and I was about to give my notice when she fell sick. I could not desert her then, of course, so I have been here much longer than I wished. And she is *not* an easy employer."

"You are well served for your mischief, Miss Forbes," he retorted unsympathetically.

Glenna pursed her lips and cocked her head at him. "My motives were pure, Lord Pontley. I admit it was a singularly worthless exercise but I felt it was my responsibility when you refused to show any pity for her. You will recall that I was then still promised to you."

"I should like to know precisely why you are no longer."

Glenna felt a flush rise to her cheeks as she remembered reading his letter to his aunt. Alarmed, Pontley groaned and muttered, "Did she subject you to her insinuations, not knowing who you were?"

It was Glenna's turn to be puzzled. "She said no more than that you had gotten yourself into a misguided engagement. I assure you it was through no words of hers that I came to my decision."

He carefully scrutinized her countenance and nodded his satisfaction. "Very well, why then did you not wait until I came to you for your answer?"

Would the truth come out if she did not tell him? It seemed likely that his aunt would allude to the letter, pleased as she was with his captivation by her niece, but would she mention that it was Glenna who had read it to her? Probably not. On the other hand, she was more than likely to convince him that she had spoken of her triumph with her companion, though Glenna had in fact discouraged any such confidences. She turned troubled blue eyes up to him and shook her head sadly. "I really do not wish to discuss it further, if you please, Lord Pontley."

Aware of her embarrassment but not of the cause of it, he relented. "If you will change into something more appropriate, I should like to dine. Is my aunt well now?"

"Yes, she's out of bed a large part of the day."

"Do you wish to avoid her, Miss Forbes?"

"If you please, I would like to go to the vicarage right away."

"After you have dined, I will drive you there." He retrieved her cap from where he had tossed it and handed it to her. "I will explain the situation to my aunt and insure that you do not meet her before you leave. Join me for dinner at five, please. I will send word to the vicarage informing them of your arrival."

Glenna murmured her agreement, stopped to retrieve the strawberry basket and fled. In her room she bathed as best she could and washed the remaining powder from her hair. It was a relief to see the natural color again, and to don an attractive gown. With her portmanteaux packed and the entry of her awful encounter with Lord Pontley duly inscribed in her journal, she descended to the drawing room, which led through sliding doors into the dining parlor. She found that Pontley had preceded her and stood gazing out the window, occupied by his thoughts and neatly dressed in a dark green coat of superfine with dove colored pantaloons. Unwilling to call his attention to herself, she quietly took a chair and sat studying her hands.

Eventually he turned from the window and started on catching sight of her. "You have allowed me to be rude, Miss Forbes. I did not hear you enter."

"I had no wish to disturb you, sir, and was perfectly content to sit for a space." With an attempt at lightness she smiled and said, "I have seldom enjoyed such a luxury in your house."

When he strode over to her, she noted that the limp was perhaps less than it had been, but she was much more aware of the tension in him than anything else. Before the intensity of his gaze she dropped her eyes and suddenly wondered what to do with her hands. "You're embarrassed for me, Miss Forbes."

Startled, her eyes flew to his face and she protested, "Nonsense. Why should I be?"

43

"Because you are familiar with the contents of a letter I wrote to my aunt."

No effort on her part could restrain the flush that crept over her face. "It is not a cause of embarrassment, my lord. Or at least, not for you. Although it was upsetting for me to have to read such a letter to your aunt, I am satisfied to be possessed of the information it contained. You can hardly expect that I would wish to have you marry me out of a sense of misdirected honor. I asked you several times at our last meeting whether you wished for me to cry off. You had only to tell me so then or at any time subsequent for me to do so with perfect amiability. The matter is settled now to our mutual satisfaction."

"Hardly," he muttered. "Misguided though your escapade has been, I can only assume that you undertook it feeling the full weight of your betrothed state, and must conclude that you had indeed intended to marry me."

"Rather the opposite, actually." Her eyes danced with amusement. "I felt certain that I would not marry you, and therefore I would never be identified to your aunt as myself."

He lifted a quizzical brow. "Then why did you come?"

"Oh, I felt sorry for your aunt. You understand, at the time I had never met her and did not realize that my sympathy was wasted. Once here, events conspired to keep me longer than I would have liked, but I put it down to my own folly. It was rather enlightening, you know, being a companion. Do you suppose I can get her to pay me?"

Pontley gave a bark of laughter. "She's ready to string you up by your thumbs, my dear Miss Forbes, but I would be more than willing to reimburse you for your time and efforts."

"You would be appalled at how little she offered me as inducement to be her companion. We pay our scullery maid a great deal more."

Dinner was announced before Pontley could respond, and he led her in to their meal feeling quite in charity with her. He had been fortunate indeed to contract an alliance with such a practical woman, who would not through any petty motive hold him to an agreement which no longer suited him. Grateful to be at last escaping from Lady Pontley, Glenna chatted throughout the meal about his aunt, the Lockwood estate and her friends at the vicarage. Her description of her arrival with the harp drew an appreciative chuckle, and he openly answered her questions about the estate in Gloucestershire. By unspoken agreement they avoided the subject of Miss Jennifer Stafford, and the meal passed off more pleasantly than either would have expected a few hours previously.

During the drive to the vicarage Pontley related his conversation with Mr. Forbes. "Was it necessary for you to be so frank with him?" Glenna protested.

"I had not intended to be, Miss Forbes, but I think you should not be so protective of him. He asked me specifically to tell you that you must not marry on his account alone."

"You don't know him as I do," she retorted. "He has been fretting himself over me."

"I don't doubt that, but I think you will find he acknowledges your right to live your life as you choose, and not be swayed by his concern for you. He will manage without your making sacrifices."

Pontley had turned to look at her and was astonished to see her face suddenly grow pale. "Are you all right, ma'am?" The horses came to a plunging halt at his insistence.

"Of course," she murmured through frozen lips. "Whyever are you stopping, Lord Pontley? You could kill your groom with a sudden stop like that." The boy behind indeed looked shaken, and Glenna used the time Pontley spoke with him to pinch her cheeks and draw a few deep breaths.

When he turned to her he thought she still looked wretched, but she urged him forward and there was nothing he could do but obey. As she seemed unable to make conversation, he turned desperately to his naval days for inspiration, and he could not be sure whether she comprehended or even heard his story of the young lieutenant from his cutter who had taken four men and rowed ashore, boarded and succeeded in floating a beached French *chassemarée* in the face of her astonished crew and a platoon of French infantry. They had arrived at the vicarage by the time he completed the tale and there was more color in her face, but he accepted the vicar's invitation of refreshment so that he would have an opportunity to see her recovered from her upset.

Phoebe eyed him warily but said nothing, and Glenna was soon chatting with her friends. To do honor to the displaced harp she played several pieces for them and Pontley wondered whether Miss Jennifer Stafford had any musical accomplishments. She had exhibited none during his visit.

On his leave-taking Glenna offered him her hand and smiled. "I hope you will be content at Lockwood, my lord, and that you can overlook my inadvised interference in your affairs."

"I accept that you meant well, Miss Forbes, and regret that your efforts were for naught." He was barely gone from the room before Phoebe drew Glenna away to her room to hear the whole story.

FIVE

Pontley spent a month at Manner Hall in Somerset attempting to sort out the management of that estate. As the furthest from Lockwood, and the smallest, it had suffered the greatest neglect. Under a blazing sun he continually rode about the acreage with the new agent, as intent on learning as on setting matters to rights. It was his intention to let the Hall itself, though its condition was not good, but he was loath to do the same at Huntley. No tenant was in the offing, however, and he had become eager to abandon the lonely life here for the more congenial atmosphere near Tetbury.

Once again, on the point of departure his destination was deflected by the receipt of a letter. His aunt wrote her usual barrage of criticism to him but near the end remarked that she had learned that Miss Forbes's father had recently died. Because of her annoyance with the young lady it seemed to give her a certain amount of satisfaction that Glenna would be suffering. Pontley felt genuine sorrow for the old man's demise; though their acquaintance had not been long, he had respected Mr. Forbes. But his greatest concern was for the daughter and her distress. He could not shake the feeling of responsibility he had come during their engagement to feel toward her, and he could not bring himself to merely send a letter of condolence. And had she not, in her kindness, gone to his aunt when she thought the old woman grieving? Probably it was absurd of him, he chided himself, but he must see her and assure himself of her well-being. There was time enough to return to Huntley to see Miss Stafford.

Glenna's circle of friends had closed around her at such a time, and Pontley arrived to find her seated with several of them in the drawing room. Her surprise when he was announced was followed by an unexpected warmth toward him for the thoughtfulness of his gesture.

There was only one man in the room with whom he was not familiar, and Glenna introduced him as the Honorable Peter Westlake. Pontley regarded the young man skeptically, taking his age to be a few years younger than himself. Westlake was dressed in the latest London fashion, with a high starched cravat and fobs hanging from each of the fob pockets on his tight, white pantaloons. He was particularly solicitous of Glenna, and Pontley took an immediate dislike to him, which was intensified when he realized that Miss Forbes's view was rather the opposite.

Pontley wished for an opportunity to speak alone with his former fiancée and, not being willing to outwait the morning's callers, he solicited a private interview. Glenna promptly excused herself and led him to the book room where the piles of letters indicated that she had received expressions of sympathy from an abundance of friends. There was one spot cleared where she had obviously been answering these condolences when she had been called away, probably for the visitors now in the drawing room.

"You will forgive the untidiness, I trust, Lord Pontley. There has been so much to do." She seated herself wearily and motioned him to a chair.

"I cannot tell you how sorry I am for your loss, Miss Forbes. I had a fond regard for your father."

"Thank you. He was fond of you, too, you know. I shall miss him." She gazed sadly out the window, lost in her own thoughts for a moment.

Pontley waited until her attention once again returned to him before he spoke. "Will you be frank with me about your circumstances now, Miss Forbes?"

"Why . . . I cannot see that they concern you, sir."

"Nevertheless, I feel concerned and would appreciate knowing how you are circumstanced. I no longer have the right to ask but I have a desire to be of what assistance I can."

"Now who is interfering?" she demanded, nervously poking the pen into the blotter.

"Your father had expected not so long ago that I would be responsible for you on his death, and I cannot believe that he would hold it amiss in me to look into your well-being. Come, Miss Forbes, let us not quibble. You must realize that but for changes in my own circumstances we would at this moment be man and wife."

"I have friends who will help me."

"I am aware of that, and if you can assure me that there is no cause for concern, I will plague you no further. But I must insist on your being honest with me. Shall you have to sell the house?"

"Yes."

"Where will you go?"

"I will take lodgings here in town, I suppose."

"Will you be able to manage on your resources without additional income?"

"Certainly."

"For how long?"

"Several years, I should imagine." Her chin was set stubbornly. "Will that be all, my lord?"

"No, Miss Forbes. I have a suggestion to make, and I pray you will not reject it outright. It has several advantages which you should weigh carefully. I have come straight from Manner Hall in Somerset, a small property with an old manor

49

house in need of some renovation. Our lack of success in finding a tenant, I fear, is entirely owing to its condition. My proposal is that you should occupy the house, rent-free, and keep an eye on the renovations which I will cause to be undertaken."

At her murmur of protest, he waved her to silence. "You would find the setting congenial, I believe, for the house is located within sight of the Bristol Channel not far from Minehead. For companionship, there are some neighbors, but you might rather choose to entertain your friends from Hastings. During your mourning period you will not wish to go into society here in any case, and the change of scene might be welcome. It will not be easy for you to see this house occupied by someone new."

Glenna regarded him bemusedly, a glint of tears in her eyes. "You are more thoughtful than I had suspected, Lord Pontley, but I must refuse your generous offer, if for no other reason than that I could not afford the staff for such a household, even were I paying no rent."

"You misunderstand, ma'am. I have to maintain some staff in any case, empty or occupied, and I would continue to do so. The manor house is a small sandstone place with gables and tall brick chimneys. The garden is especially charming, and the lawns are lush, if unkempt. My agent will be fully occupied in seeing to the farming and forestry; I cannot spare him to supervise the renovations to the house. The impressions you expressed with regard to Lockwood encourage me to think that you would succeed in the task admirably."

"I appreciate your confidence, but I really cannot accept. You must see that I can take nothing from you, sir." She poked the pen into the blotter once again and was startled when he grasped her hand.

"Stop that. I sympathize with your distress, Miss Forbes, but I am impatient with your lack of realism. You will need something to occupy your mind, to keep you busy, for the next few months, and I can think of nothing better than my proposition."

Glenna shook his hand off and deposited the pen on the desk. "Well, naturally *you* cannot. I don't need you dictating to me, Lord Pontley; I am perfectly capable of managing for myself."

He shrugged exasperatedly. "I know that, ma'am. But I am offering you a change of scene, an occupation, a chance to entertain your friends with no expense." He rose and paced about the room, the limp scarcely noticeable now. "Conserve your resources, Miss Forbes, until you need to call upon them."

"We are not discussing naval strategy, my lord, but my life."

She was subjected to his penetrating gaze. "And if you spend your all within the next few years, what will you do then? Go to live with some relation? You would be in no better position than you were with my aunt."

"My relations are not so absurd as yours," she retorted. "There is . . . another possibility arisen."

He studied her until the color mounted to her cheeks. "That young man—Westmore?"

"Westlake."

"Who is he?"

"Lady Garth's son, third out of five."

"And where did he spring from?" he asked shortly.

"I have known Peter for some time. That is, I knew him some time ago, though I have not seen him for six years or so," she replied stiffly.

"If you didn't want him six years ago, I wouldn't take him

now! He can only have gotten worse. My God, he must have a perpetual stiff neck from wearing that ridiculous cravat."

"It is the height of fashion," she replied defensively. Her voice dropped to a whisper. "And I did want him six years ago."

He stopped his pacing and turned to face her. "Then why didn't you have him?"

"Because. . . ." She could not continue.

"He didn't ask you."

"He did! Oh, leave me alone. This is none of your business in any case. I do not have to answer to you for anything."

"Certainly not," he said amiably, "but I should like to know. Did it have something to do with the insinuations my aunt made?"

Glenna rose and drew herself up to her full height. "I have no idea what insinuations your detestable aunt may have made, but I can only consider you paltry to have listened to anything said against your fiancée."

"Ah, but I didn't listen to them, my dear Miss Forbes, though I was burning with curiosity. Let me see, before I shut her up she had managed to cast aspersions on your paternity and hinted at something irregular in your one season in London. No doubt that was when you met Westlake."

"Go away."

"And then there was the most remarkable effect that evening I drove you to the vicarage when I suggested that you had no need to make sacrifices for your father." This time he thought she would faint and, disgusted with himself, he hastened to lower her into a chair. "Forgive me. God knows I did not come here to torment you, Miss Forbes." He chafed her hands, murmuring apologies. "I will leave you, but I beg that you will accept my offer of Manner Hall. Even if you are to wed, it cannot be for some time and I truly believe you would enjoy it there."

Glenna roused herself to contemplate him, where he crouched beside her chair. "If you were so curious about me, why did you not ask me? Were you willing to marry someone whose background might reflect ill on you?"

"I don't see how it could have. Your father I knew to be an admirable man; your friends accepted you without reservation. If other gentlemen who knew you far better than I were desirous to marry you, then they must not believe any the worse of you. Had our engagement continued, I might have taxed you for some information, but only so that I would be aware of our strengths and weaknesses."

"Do you always see life in terms of a naval battle, Lord Pontley?" she asked curiously.

His grin was infectious. "I am a practical man, Miss Forbes. What needs to be done, I do. It would be foolish of me to put myself at a disadvantage through false delicacy, don't you think?"

"No doubt." Glenna rose and walked to a small mahogany secretaire from which she extracted a yellowing letter. "If you will read this, you will understand the whole of your aunt's insinuations."

Pontley refused the proffered item. "Thank you, no, Miss Forbes. I have no right to do so now, and I have no wish to further upset you."

"It can only comfort me for you to read it, my lord, for it vindicates my mother most effectively, I believe."

"I will accept your word for that, ma'am."

"I don't want you to accept my word, sir; I want you to read the letter." She continued to hold it out to him until he was forced to take it.

Before doing so he studied her determined face, made a gesture of resignation and walked to the window where he could better discern the faded writing. The letter was dated 23 June 1797, and it was from Lady Garth.

My dear Miss Forbes [it began], It is with a great deal of sorrow that I write you, and I would not do so were it not essential. I have watched with trepidation the growth of affection between you and my son Peter for some months now, and have not found the courage to speak with you. For myself, I would welcome you as a daughter into my family with great warmth were it not for some circumstances in the past of which I cannot believe you are cognizant. When your mother (dear Lady Harriet) married your father it was to the disappointment of my husband, who had courted her assiduously. He had been convinced that his consequence was so much greater than your father's that she would not throw away such an opportunity. You must understand, dear Miss Forbes, that I am well aware of the ancient lineage of your father's family, and by no means regard it lightly. Nonetheless, Lord Garth felt that his title, wealth and person were such as your mother could not refuse. He was sadly disillusioned and did not marry me until some years afterward.

Your parents seldom came to town, being quite content, I suppose, with life in Hastings. However, when your aunt, Lady Mary, was to be married, they came to London for the season in '78. Although I had then been married to Lord Garth for some years, and had produced three sons for him, he made an utter fool of himself by pursuing your mother quite relentlessly during their stay, much as Sheridan does Lady B. now, but with much less success. There would have been no gossip, and in fact was none at the time because your mother was so obviously devoted to your father, and was consistently cold to Lord Garth. However, your parents had been married for many years by this time without any offspring, and the following winter your mother gave birth to you.

Now, I know for a fact that my husband had no success with your mother (for he is wont to proclaim his triumphs to me), and that the timing of your birth was a matter of coincidence. But it was an unfortunate coincidence, and such as made lovely *on dit* for months in London. So you see, child, there is a rumor abroad that Lord Garth is your father, and it is the greatest ill luck that you and my son should form an attachment. (Not that for yourself it should cause any hindrance in any case, my dear, for Lord Garth is positively *not* Peter's father.)

At this point Lord Pontley interrupted his reading to mutter, "What a menagerie!" The letter continued:

Your father, however, was much distressed by these rumors. He did not for a moment believe them—I have never seen such a loving couple as your parents, my dear. Perhaps it has something to do with their never coming to London . . . No matter. What I am trying to say, Miss Forbes, is that an alliance between you and Peter would be most abhorrent to your father, bringing back painful memories, and giving rise to the most vicious gossip here. I could not, of course, in my position, endeavor to allay such rumors. I hope you can understand that. Your devotion to your father is well known, especially since your mother's death last year, and I felt in explaining all this to you I might prevent you from hurting him deeply. You must do as you wish, of course, but I could not allow you to act without an understanding of the background of the matter. It is a pity that the indiscretion of your elders should cause you heartbreak, dear Miss Forbes, but so it ever has been, I fear. I would be overwhelmingly grateful if you would write to me and apprise me of your sentiments in this instance. Yours, etc.

"If it were not so pathetic," Pontley commented, "it would be laughable." He set the letter on the secretaire with a distasteful gesture. "Is Westlake familiar with the contents?"

"Yes, of course. We discussed the matter at the time and agreed to part."

"You realize that nothing has changed except your father's death. There would still be gossip if you married him."

"He does not seem to mind, and I certainly do not. My father can no longer be hurt by such maliciousness, and that was always my only concern."

"And Westlake has waited all this time for you?"

A shadow passed over Glenna's face. "No, Lord Pontley, he has not, but on the other hand he has not married and maintains his desire to do so now."

"Admirable, I'm sure, but I hope you will take the time to get to know him again, Miss Forbes. A man changes over six years."

"I intend no precipitate action, my lord, you may be sure," she replied coolly.

"Do not freeze me now, Miss Forbes. I am gratified by your confidence and wish only for your happiness and comfort. If you will undertake my commission at Manner Hall I will be perfectly satisfied. Please grant me that one indulgence for the sake of my peace of mind."

Although she hesitated, Glenna was tempted by the offer. It would indeed be difficult for her to remain in Hastings at this time, with all its memories of her father. Her movements would be restricted by her mourning, and she envisioned days passing by purposelessly. The project itself was fascinating to her, and she felt sure that many of her friends would be willing to visit—including Peter. She was not in the habit of accepting such largesse, however, and if she did undertake the supervision of the renovation she intended to do it thoroughly.

"Are there any horses?" she asked suddenly.

Startled, Pontley nodded. "Only a few. Do you ride?"

"Being town-bred does not necessarily preclude such a skill," she retorted haughtily, but her eyes danced mischievously. "I have never been on an animal more active than a donkey, but I should like to learn."

"Excellent. I will send word that you are to be expected within the month, but you had best give a few days' notice yourself."

"I had not actually accepted yet," she protested.

"Well, do so and I will allow you to return to your friends. You have kept them waiting far too long already."

"Very well," she sighed. "Please believe that I am grateful to you, Lord Pontley."

"There is no need for gratitude. I am satisfied that your father would be pleased. And now, if you will excuse me to your friends, I will be on my way. You have only to write if there is a problem. I will be at Huntley for a while and will advise you when I depart for Lockwood."

"And the renovations? Have you left instructions with your agent?"

"He will have them by the time you arrive, Miss Forbes." Pontley mentally noted that his agent would be vastly surprised at this turn of events, but he was committed now to follow through with it, and he did not regret his actions.

SIX

The sale of Glenna's house in Hastings was accomplished quickly through the office of friends of hers. She included most of the furniture but retained those items which seemed especially memorable, in spite of the carter's charges she would have to pay to have them taken to Minehead. Her friend Phoebe had agreed to accompany her, as Glenna had found situations for all of the servants, another parting which had caused her distress. The activity, though, had occupied her mind and her time, for which she could but be grateful. Two days before she and Phoebe were to set out there was a note from Pontley advising her that a civilian captain who was a friend of his would be willing to take the ladies and their belongings on board on his way to Bristol. The journey, Pontley wrote, would be quicker, less expensive, and interesting for her. She would have to be ready on the Wednesday, however, rather than the following day she had mentioned in her note as her starting date.

Going by sea had never occurred to Glenna, and the thought frankly horrified her, but Phoebe was delighted with the idea and pressed home the advantage of monetary savings.

"But my harp will probably be ruined by the salty air," Glenna protested.

"I dare say it will survive as well as it did in that post chaise," her friend responded dryly. "How can you not wish to go by sea? You very nearly married a captain in the Royal Navy, Glenna."

"He did not make it a condition of our marriage that I ever come on board a ship."

"Well, you would have had to, you know. I met a Mrs. Fremantle last autumn in St. Helens whose husband is a captain on the *Ganges*. She spoke of being on board frequently, and told me that the previous day the Prince of Wales had drunk six glasses of cherry brandy at luncheon with her husband, plus a bottle of mulled port wine. Imagine!"

"I can easily imagine, my dear Phoebe, and I fear the only way I could get through a sea voyage would be on six glasses of cherry brandy for each meal."

"Don't be a goose, love. Please say we may. I shall probably never have the opportunity again."

"Very well, but I give you fair warning I will as like as not be ill the entire passage."

Captain Andrews was startled by the amount of baggage he was expected to take on for the ladies, but he ignored the inconvenience with a cavalier shrug of his shoulders and settled Glenna and Phoebe into a large cabin with a fireplace and two comfortable cots designed to prevent motion. They sailed with a fair wind and a calm sea which quickly reassured Glenna, and she soon found herself intrigued by the voyage.

Phoebe took to sketching the scenes they passed, and Captain Andrews willingly provided information on Eastbourne and Brighton, the Isle of Wight and St. Alban's Head. They took dinner with the captain, who dined in splendor and assured them that he had been to no special trouble for the meal.

"When you spend as much time at sea as I do, you learn to make yourself as comfortable on board as you would at home. And the little touches of civilization take on extra importance. You have no idea how lonely a man gets when he is at sea for weeks on end, often out of sight of land, with nothing but his own thoughts and monotonous duties."

"Have you a family to go home to, Captain Andrews?" Glenna asked.

"No, ma'am, but I have a comfortable little house near Weston-super-Mare and my brother and his family live hard by. The children love to come on board and climb over everything, talking twelve to the dozen and asking more questions than could be answered in a fortnight." He smiled approvingly. "I think the eldest lad will take to the sea; perhaps the youngest as well."

Phoebe caught Glenna's eye mischievously and offered, "Miss Forbes is very accomplished on the harp, Captain Andrews, and I am sure if you were to have the harp brought from our cabin she would play for you."

"Would you indeed, Miss Forbes? Hobart . . . that is, Lord Pontley had mentioned last spring that you play exquisitely."

Glenna very nearly said that it was the reason he had offered for her, but on second thought decided such a remark might make the good captain uncomfortable. He seemed wary of her, while he was completely at ease with Phoebe, and Glenna could only assume that, not knowing the basis of the broken engagement, he did not wish to make a misstep.

The harp was brought and Glenna willingly entertained them for an hour, since Phoebe teased her that she had not touched the instrument during its stay at the vicarage. "And Papa never did understand why you brought it for a one-night stay and then left it with us for a month."

"He probably prayed for the expected invasion so that the French would relieve him of it," Glenna retorted.

"Pooh! He merely wished that you would return so that it need not sit silent." Phoebe turned to the captain. "May we walk on the deck?"

He escorted them, and Glenna fell behind, lost in the

wonder of the water lapping against the ship, the pin-pricks of the stars in the dark, moonless canopy above them. Instinctively she thought that she must write her father to tell him of the amazing experience, and brought herself up sharply. Consigning a description to her journal would not be the same, but she could write to Pontley and thank him; Peter, she thought, had never been on a ship and would not understand. She was recalled from her thoughts only when the other two returned to seek her, talking as though they had known each other for years rather than hours. The captain's dark hair and ruggedly handsome countenance provided a perfect complement to Phoebe's fair hair and skin, her delicate features and her elegant carriage. Their laughter warmed Glenna, and she set aside her sadness.

The journey was relatively uneventful, with only one storm encountered off Land's End, and even this proved awe-inspiring rather than terrifying to the two ladies. The calm efficiency of the sailors and the unwavering good humor of Captain Andrews, convinced Glenna that they were not indeed likely to disappear beneath the angry lashings of the waves and rain. On the third day they were delivered to shore in Porlock Bay, none the worse for the experience. In fact, much the richer, and, Glenna thought with delight, in possession of a new friend. Captain Andrews had shown a marked interest in Phoebe and begged permission to visit them once they were settled.

The Manner Hall staff had arranged for a cart to await their arrival and transport the baggage and furniture, and the ladies were bundled into an ancient carriage drawn by two very unlikely-looking animals. "I don't doubt they are used on the farm," Glenna sighed. "And Pontley only convinced me to come by assuring me that there were a few horses to ride. I had hoped you would teach me."

"Not on either of those," Phoebe protested.

"Never mind. There will be other things to do."

Darkness had fallen before they reached the Hall, and they could tell little about the estate. The hall into which they were ushered was rather shabby, but clean, and the servants were lined up to greet them. Just as though I were the mistress, Glenna thought with amusement, until she realized that was indeed how they intended to treat her. Mrs. Morgan, the housekeeper, identified her husband as the butler, their son as the footman, their daughter as the cook and a niece as kitchen help. The daughter's husband was in charge of the stables—such as they were, Glenna thought wryly. The only unrelated person was a housemaid, who, from the flattering glances she cast at the footman, Glenna judged to be soon a member of the family.

There was a motion at the door and a robust young man entered. "Excuse me, Miss Forbes. I only now received word that you had arrived."

"This is Mr. Glover, the agent, Miss Forbes," Mrs. Morgan pronounced doubtfully. Glenna could not be sure whether the woman eyed him askance as an outsider, or for himself.

The housekeeper's opinion did not seem to perturb the young man, who assured Glenna that he was at her service. She liked his frank brown eyes and open countenance, the look of stolid country stock about him. "I'm pleased to meet you, Mr. Glover. Has Lord Pontley communicated with you on the renovations for the Hall?"

"Well, so to speak, ma'am. Not very specific, was he. If I might wait on you in the morning, you could perhaps make more of it than I."

Glenna had the distinct impression that the young man

was amused by his instructions but she merely agreed to meet with him at ten.

"And now, ma'am," Mrs. Morgan hastened to interject, "you must be weary from your journey and wish to be shown your room. My Betsey will have a warm supper for you whenever you wish and Alice will assist you and Miss Thomas." She gave a curt nod of dismissal to the younger members of the staff and herself led the two newcomers up the finely carved oak staircase.

"If there's a thing you wish and don't find to hand, you have only to let me know. On the other hand, if you don't see it, we probably don't have it, but never mind. Lord Pontley wrote as how we was to keep you comfortable and so we shall, if I have anything to say about matters, and I promise you I do. Proper delighted we are to have folks in residence. The late Lord Pontley never came next or nigh the place from one year to the next, though we did have occasion to house his friends from time to time. Not always the best-behaved gentlemen they were, begging your pardon, ma'am, but then it's no more than the truth. This is your room, Miss Forbes, with Miss Thomas direct across the hall. The fires haven't been lit here for some time, so it may be the least bit smoky for a while."

She bustled into the room and cast a quick, approving glance about. "Alice will bring you a can of hot water right off. If you've a mind to rest for a bit, my Betsey will keep your supper warm, but the sooner you partake of a bite, the sooner you feel restored, I always say."

Phoebe shared an amused look with her friend; Mrs. Morgan obviously took her own advice, for she was the roundest, most comfortable-looking woman Phoebe had seen in some time. The room relegated to Phoebe was similar to, if not quite so large, as Glenna's. Although well-proportioned, the wall coverings were faded and the furniture scuffed. When Glenna peeped in to urge Phoebe down to supper, she commented, "Lord Pontley did not exaggerate the necessity for some renovation, did he?"

"I think he underestimated, if anything, from what you have told me. Didn't you say he had actively sought for a tenant?"

"Yes; absurd, isn't it? I cannot imagine who would consider such a scruffy place. The fact that it is clean is its only saving grace," Glenna remarked dryly.

They supped on rabbits smothered with onions and pike served with a sauce compounded of anchovy sauce, walnut pickle and melted butter. The currant pudding in addition won their approval, and they pronounced Betsey a welcome inmate in the household. "Every bit as fine as Captain Andrews's table," Phoebe remarked.

"We shall have to search out the kitchen in the morning, but frankly, I am exhausted and very nearly asleep on my feet." Glenna rose and, unable to suppress a yawn, shook her head remorsefully. "No doubt it is all that sea air. I am grateful you convinced me to come by water, Phoebe, as I enjoyed it tremendously."

"No more than I, I promise you. We were fortunate to have such an amiable gentleman as Captain Andrews to escort us." Phoebe joined her friend at the door but did not meet her eyes.

Glenna pressed her hand gently. "I think we will see more of Captain Andrews, my dear."

SEVEN

Glenna's visit to the kitchen was an eye-opener. She found it difficult to believe that the delectable meal they had partaken of the previous evening had been produced in this dark, smoky hole. The turnspit looked medieval, the open fire on a hearth too small to cook for above a dozen people, with the kettle for the hot water supply absorbing the majority of its space. There was no stove. The Forbeses had had a Bodley range for the two years since it had been introduced, and prided themselves on the modernness of their kitchen. Glenna was appalled by the lack of equipment at Manner: only one boiler and two stew-pans, with no covers. The frying pan was untinned and there was only one copper ladle and one saucepan. She began to make notes of the necessities, consulting with the astonished Betsey, who was all eagerness to assure her that she would be delighted with a modernization of her sphere. It was through no hesitation on *her* part that the kitchens were so ill-equipped.

"You manage amazingly well on so little," Glenna confided to her, "but if Lord Pontley expects to find a suitable tenant, he must realize that this kitchen cannot by any means serve up an elegant dinner party. It confounds me that you can serve more than the staff from that miserable hearth. Surely previous generations could have managed no better."

Betsey gave a despairing gesture. "The previous viscount had the bake house torn down. Not that I blame him, for it was falling apart and blackened beyond recall, I fear. But he made no effort to restore the ovens and hearth lost."

"Well, we will just have to make it right, won't we? Where do you bake your bread?"

"In the cottage, ma'am. John carries about for me sometimes, there not being much activity in the stables."

"A most haphazard arrangement at best. Certainly there will have to be ovens here. You cannot be expected to improvise to such a degree. I won't hold you further, Betsey, except to tell you how much we enjoyed our supper, and to assure you that Miss Thomas and I expect nothing elaborate. I hope to provide you with better facilities shortly."

But her interview with Mr. Glover was not encouraging so far as the kitchen was concerned. He had brought with him the letter he had received from Pontley and offered it to her almost despairingly. Glenna perused the brief contents: "Glover—Miss Forbes will be arriving to stay at the Hall. I have asked that she oversee the necessary renovations. What is needed: repair of slate roof, upkeep of grounds, painting of interior rooms, and for God's sake have a water closet put in. You may use one-third of the net estate revenues for these projects. And get her a horse. Pontley."

Glennna stared at the sketchy instructions for a moment before meeting the amused glint in Glover's eyes. "But what of the kitchen? Or the draperies? Does he not see that the floors are scuffed and the furniture disgraceful?"

"All beside the point, I fear, ma'am. One-third of the net revenues at this point might possibly cover the repair of the roof and the water closet. The harvest will be adequate, but nothing to write home about. I've just begun to plan the four course rotation, but there is still drainage to be done, and the proper equipment to be purchased for adequate cultivation. I fear Lord Pontley has only a minimal idea of the expenses involved."

"Well, you needn't buy the horse, at any rate."

"I already have, Miss Forbes. He was very specific about that."

"You must return it, then. I won't be a drain on the estate for a luxury."

"Quite a bargain I made on the little mare, ma'am. You'll find you need her to get about the estate and keep an eye on matters."

"But I barely know how to ride," Glenna protested, "and without a mount for Miss Thomas, there is absolutely no purpose in having one for me."

"Now, that can be easily managed. No trouble to stable one of mine here for her use. I can't ride more than one at a time," he remarked with a grin. "No need to fret over the horse, ma'am. It's the other expenses I cannot see how to cover."

"Is there no way other than the crops to increase the revenues?"

"Not without additional staff—a gardener, a gamekeeper, a dairy maid."

"I fear I am no more familiar with the workings of an estate than Lord Pontley," Glenna confessed. "How would they increase the revenues?"

"A gardener to produce our own kitchen vegetables, herbs and such, with any excess sold in Minehead. I understand there has been no outdoor staff here for some time and we purchase necessities in town. Mrs. Morgan has kept the closest parterre tidy, but she won't have time for that now."

"Would a gardener pay for himself?"

Glover considered the question carefully and then shook his head. "No, ma'am, but having him would provide the resource for keeping up the grounds. Then there would be no additional expense."

"Very well, of what use is a gamekeeper?"

"The estate is overrun with rabbits—destructive to the crops, and one of the few game items the estate could sell. The hedgerows are cover for woodcock and quails, too. Now a gamekeeper, he'd more than pay for himself, ma'am, and any excess could be spent on the renovations."

Glenna noted this on her growing list. "A dairy maid?"

"John has looked after the dairy as well as the stables, but just enough to keep it swilled down for a minimum of production. Now, with our herd we could be getting cheese and cream enough to sell in town as well. A dairy maid would more than pay her own way."

"Have we the churns and pans?"

"They're there, ma'am. Hardly used these last years but more than adequate."

"I shall write to Lord Pontley today with your suggestions. Should you think of any further possibilities, please inform me." She sighed exasperatedly. "I know so little about country estates and their possibilities."

"You might find some books here in the library, ma'am. Though it is far from a complete collection, the main portion is on animal husbandry and estate management."

Glenna looked about the walls, carelessly strewn with ancient volumes. "Yes, I can see hours of pleasure before me."

Mr. Glover chuckled appreciatively. "Lord Pontley said much the same, ma'am."

"No doubt."

Manner Hall
15 August 1804

My dear Lord Pontley: Miss Thomas and I have arrived safely at Manner Hall after a most enjoyable voyage by water. I am appreciative of your kindness in arranging for our passage, and your thoughtfulness in the expense and time we saved. Captain Andrews proved an entertaining and informative escort; we hope to see him once we are settled in here.

As to matters on the estate, I am not so sanguine. Mr. Glover informs me that the amount you suggested would possibly cover the roof repair and water closet. I gather the latter is a rather expensive operation. The upkeep of the grounds and the painting of the interior rooms could not be covered. I am sensible of the usefulness, in fact the necessity, for the roof repair and water closet but must feel that the other items are almost equally important. Perhaps you did not visit the kitchen during your stay. I assure you no self-respecting gentleman would let a house with such a miserable hole—so dark and ill-equipped. I would give it priority over the grounds, even over the interior painting. Your predecessor had the bake house torn down but not replaced. That alone is vital to the functioning of a gentleman's house, to say nothing of the need for a range.

In an effort to find some resources not currently available from your estate, Mr. Glover has suggested the services of a gardener, gamekeeper and dairy maid. The latter two would more than compensate for their wages, and the former would partially do so, as well as making a start on the upkeep of the grounds.

I would appreciate your approval of these plans, as I am anxious to fulfill my commission here.

Your obedient servant, Glenna Forbes

P.S. Thank you for the horse.

Huntley

20 August 1804

My dear Miss Forbes: I am pleased that you have arrived safely at Manner and enjoyed your trip. It is with some reluctance that I give my permission for you to hire a gardener, gamekeeper and dairy maid, for I cannot see that a town-bred young lady will know how to supervise their activities and I have no intention of sparing Glover from his duties to assist you. Do not think that I do not appreciate the effort you are making, but I would rather that you did not get beyond your depth. You may use any profits from these activities for those improvements I outlined to Glover. I cannot understand the importance you attach to the kitchen; perhaps it is a bugbear with you, but I would appreciate your restraint in my house. I wish you luck in learning to ride.

Yours, etc., Pontley

"A bugbear!" Glenna exclaimed on receipt of this missive. "Can you believe him, Phoebe? Where does he think his meals come from—the stables?"

"You must remember that it *is* his house, Glenna. If he doesn't wish to improve the kitchen, there is nothing you can do about it."

Glenna's face was set stubbornly. "Pontley commissioned me to supervise the work so that he might obtain a tenant. I cannot believe he will get one with the kitchen in its present condition."

"Let him find that out later, love."

"But, Phoebe, he has provided me with a house and a horse and I would feel remiss if I didn't succeed in his purpose."

"You are too conscientious by half, Glenna. Let it be."

But Glenna could not feel at ease over the situation. Interspersed with the new duties she assumed, and the riding lessons Phoebe gladly offered, she sat down with the books in the library, searching for a solution. Her head was soon spinning with animal husbandry, crop rotation, butter churning and game statutes. Phoebe insisted on excursions to Minehead and Selworthy, proclaiming her friend a very dull companion indeed with her nose forever in a book. The excursions proved more useful than Glenna expected.

Manner Hall
30 August 1804

Lord Pontley: I have studied the various possibilities and ask your permission to institute several new activities here, with an end toward providing funds for the kitchen renovation. There is a flourishing basket-making industry in Minehead and we find that we would be able to provide rushes for this work to the village women with some profit to the estate. I should like also to increase the poultry so that the eggs and chickens may provide additional revenue. Since there can be no importation of partridge eggs from France during the current state of affairs, I should like your permission to institute a small enterprise in that line as well. Your answer will be eagerly awaited.

Yours, etc., Glenna Forbes

Huntley
4 September 1804

Miss Forbes: You are defeating my purpose in sending

71

you to Manner Hall. There is no need for you to exhaust yourself in such activities as you enumerate for my edification. For God's sake, woman, all I had in mind was for you to keep an eye on the work going forward— surely a simple task. I do not refuse my permission for your activities, but I hope you will think better of them. The kitchen seemed perfectly adequate to me; my meals there were far better than I receive here.

Yours, etc., Pontley

"There, I told you he had no idea of what a kitchen should be," Glenna proclaimed triumphantly as she waved the letter in her friend's face. "He thought the kitchen perfectly adequate! Imagine! If Betsey were not a wonder, we would have no meals at all."

"Captain Andrews will be here any moment," Phoebe reminded her. "Had you best not change now?"

"Of course. Forgive me for ranting so." She turned to go but stopped. "He did not refuse his permission, though, so I suppose I may do as I wish."

Phoebe sighed. "Glenna, I will be very upset if you are not dressed by the time Captain Andrews arrives."

"Yes, yes. I am going."

Captain Andrews had arranged for them to visit Dunster Castle, since the Luttrells were not presently in residence. He had had shipping commissions from John Luttrell over the years and the housekeeper, an amiable woman, showed them about the main apartments. Phoebe was delighted with the captain's knowledge of the house and its contents, for he had been there before. The inner hall formed the nucleus of the house, with its spider's web ceiling and overmantel decorated with the arms of Thomas Luttrell and his wife Margaret

Hadley, one of the few commoners to have heraldic sup-
porters.

The Great Parlor was paneled as well, with an elaborate
plaster ceiling; its recessed square center with a quatrefoil
panel framed by a rib decorated with leaves, flowers and fruit
caused Phoebe to murmur, "Just what we need at Manner
Hall, Glenna. Perhaps you should write Lord Pontley. The
acanthus leaf scrolls would surely attract a tenant."

"She mocks me, Captain Andrews. I vow I have not the
least intention of going beyond what is necessary at Manner,
my dear Phoebe . . . and the kitchen is necessary."

But it was after they had studied the allegorical portrait of
Sir John Luttrell and the almost equally fascinating "Portrait
of a Young Cavalier," that an idea occurred to Glenna and
she mused, "Now that is what we need."

Phoebe had been studying the extravagant costume and
asked, "What is that, my dear? A fancy dress ball?"

"See his boots? What do they remind you of?"

"They look as though two enormous butterflies had set
down on them," Phoebe laughed.

"Precisely. And that reminded me of bees. I think I shall
keep some bees."

"Good Lord, you cannot be serious," Captain Andrews
exclaimed. "Why ever would you do such a thing?"

"We could sell the honey."

And so when they returned to the Hall and Phoebe
strolled through the gardens with Captain Andrews, Glenna
took pen in hand.

Manner Hall
15 September 1804

Most Honored Landlord: The renovations proceed very

well and though the work for the drain pipes causes an enormous amount of dust which quite oversets Mrs. Morgan, the progress is excellent. The roof is already mended and the grounds are looking better. It will take some time to make them entirely presentable, of course, but I consider the improvement little short of miraculous. I should like your permission to keep bees.

Yours, etc., Glenna Forbes

Huntley
22 September 1804

Ambitious tenant: You have it, God help me.

Yours, etc. Pontley

It was some time before Glenna was able to undertake her latest project, as friends had come to visit. There were excursions made to the picturesque villages of Luccombe and Allerford, as well as walks on the moor and rides through the Horner Woods. From Dunkery Hill they could see the distant hills of Wales across the channel and watch the skylarks drift over the golden brown trees.

Peter Westlake arrived a week after the other guests and Glenna found her time much occupied with him. There was no time to think of bees when she had his company on top of her other duties about the estate.

When they rode out one day Peter was impressed with her recently acquired skill of riding. "You have a good seat for a beginner. Is the mare your own?"

"Oh, no, Pontley got her for me, and I must say I'm very fond of her. Most days I find it necessary to ride out to speak

74

with the gamekeeper or see the progress of the further gardens, so learning to ride became essential."

"This viscount . . . Well, I suppose I have no right to ask."

Glenna reined in her mount under a stand of trees, where he joined her. "You may ask me anything you wish about him, Peter."

"Mother told me you were engaged to him last winter, but he was a naval captain then, of course. Did he expect to come into the viscountcy?"

"No, far from it. His cousin William died in the spring, and shortly afterwards they received word that the younger brother, Keith, had been killed in India last autumn."

"So it did not matter to you that he wouldn't have a title."

Glenna regarded him perplexedly. "No, why should it?"

"I have much less chance than he of ever having a title," he replied stiffly. "Both of my older brothers already have sons."

"I'm sure I'm happy for them." She grinned and pushed the curls away from her eyes. "You must know I don't give a fig about such things as titles, Peter."

"Then why were you going to marry him? That is . . . all these years you have not become engaged . . ."

"Do you want to know if I was attached to him?" she asked gently.

Peter refused to meet her gaze but stared stolidly at the channel some distance away. When he did not speak, Glenna continued, "I hardly knew Pontley, really, but he seemed a good man. Father fretted that I would not be well provided for when he died, and his fondest wish was that I would have the security of marriage."

"If you are saying that you became engaged to him for your father's sake, then why did you break the engagement?" Peter's tone indicated that he did not believe her.

Although irritated by his incredulity, she answered him

evenly. "There were many reasons for crying off, Peter. I was not particularly pleased with his abandoning his naval career, though I could understand the necessity. Mostly, though, in the end I terminated the engagement because I had reason to believe he had formed an attachment elsewhere and felt hampered by our arrangement."

"And is he engaged to someone else now?"

"I suppose so, though I have not been officially informed. He writes only of estate matters, and very briefly."

"You seem to take a deal of trouble with his estate."

The accusatory tone snapped her resolve to be patient. "I am enjoying my commission here, Peter, and have every intention of fulfilling it as best I can. Would you have me sitting in lodgings in Hastings moping about all day? I had very little knowledge of the countryside when I came and am fascinated to be learning more each day."

"Perhaps you would not be comfortable living in London now," he retorted.

Unwilling to come to grips with the significance of his remark when she was feeling exasperated with him, she turned away. Her eye was caught by a movement in the undergrowth of the copse and in a moment she had leaped down from the mare and trod lightly to the spot. "Oh, look, Peter, it's a tiny deer. I think he's wounded."

Her companion, who had begun to feel uneasy with their conversation, was willing to abandon it on any pretext and joined her where she was crouched by the spotted baby deer. "Looks like he's taken a ball in his leg."

"We'll take him to the stables and see to it."

"For God's sake, Glenna, how do you think we'd get him there?"

"I thought," she said slowly, her eyes lifting to meet his, "that you could carry him, but if you do not wish to soil your clothes, I shall carry him myself."

Peter drew her to her feet and then leaned down to pick up the struggling deer without a word. They walked silently back to their horses, where Peter was faced with the problem of mounting handicapped by the bulky animal, who in its terror continually struck out with his tiny hoofs at various places on Peter's body. When Glenna could no longer restrain her amusement at the sight, she burst out laughing, and though his brow grew thunderous at first, in a moment he sheepishly joined in her mirth. The little creature grew still in the face of his hilarity and Peter laid him on the ground while he handed Glenna onto her horse. "Can you hold him for a moment while I mount?"

"It's the least I can do," she murmured, her eyes still dancing, and accepted the now-quiescent animal in her arms.

Their journey to the stables was slow, but peace was restored between them and they spoke easily on indifferent subjects. Glenna was relieved to find that Peter was not devoid of a sense of humor after all, and the ability to laugh at himself. She had begun to fear that his years in the metropolis had made him rigid, a slave to the cult of fashion and a dilettante. Pontley's advice echoed in her mind, but she refused to credit him with the searching study she was making of her prospective suitor. After all, who took advice on matters of the heart from a man so smitten that he wrote of elfin charm and winsomeness? Glenna was well aware that the six years which separated her from her original infatuation were critical ones, and she had no intention of making up her mind until she was thoroughly familiar with this older Peter.

The advent of a deer into his stables did not discompose John Booker in the least. With an adeptness which impressed Glenna, he removed the ball and cleaned the wound. "I reckon he'll be right as rain in a few days, ma'am. Would you have me keep him here?"

"If it's not too inconvenient. I should not like to see him set free before he has the strength to fend for himself." Glenna turned to Peter and smiled. "There, we have done our good deed for the day and deserve a scrumptious tea which I have no doubt Betsey will have ready." She placed her hand on his arm and they returned companionably to the Hall where Phoebe met them at the door of the drawing room.

"Captain Andrews has come, Glenna, and I have invited him to tea. Caroline and Ralph were watching from the window for you and said you brought a *deer* to the stables." Phoebe obviously did not credit this tale until she saw the disheveled state of Peter's clothing. He immediately excused himself to change.

"He's the most adorable thing, Phoebe. John took a ball from his leg and says he'll be fine in a few days."

An astonished look greeted this statement before Phoebe said, "Oh, the deer."

Glenna giggled. "Did you think I meant Peter, my dear? Well, he was adorable, too, standing there holding the little creature while it kicked him unmercifully. Let me change, Phoebe, and I'll be with you in a moment."

The group she joined did not include Mr. Westlake as yet, since his sartorial perfection was a matter of pride with him, and took some time to accomplish. Caroline and Ralph Carmichael, her friends from Bristol who had come to visit, were discussing sailing with the captain. Glenna greeted Captain Andrews with a warm smile, as she had not seen him since the day of their excursion to Dunster Castle.

"And have you set up your bees?" he quizzed her.

Guiltily she confessed that she had been too busy to do so, but reassured him that she had every intention of embarking on the project in the near future.

"I doubt it's the right time of year for bees, in any case," he comforted her, with a laughing glance at Phoebe. "The flowers will not last more than another month."

Glenna considered this remark thoughtfully. "I should like to get started, though. Mrs. Morgan's brother has offered us whatever we need and I have Pontley's permission."

"Such as it was," Phoebe laughed. "And not a book in the place on beekeeping," she sighed.

"Pontley probably took all the really useful books with him," Glenna retorted.

Captain Andrews agreed to dine with them, and Glenna played the harp for her small circle in the evening. She was aware that Peter was restless during her recital and remembered that, unlike Pontley, he showed no interest in her accomplishment. It was unfortunate but not oversetting, as she had other interests; still, she considered her performance her only skill and regretted that Peter should think it so negligible.

EIGHT

Having been reminded of her purpose, Glenna proceeded the next day to acquire the bees.

Manner Hall

5 October 1804

Dear Lord Pontley: Glenna has asked that I write you, as she is unable to do so at this point. She wished to advise you that the water closet has been installed and the painting of the interior rooms will be started this week. Within the next two months she believes there will be sufficient funds to begin work on the kitchen, and hopes that you are still in agreement with this undertaking.

Glenna will *not* be keeping bees, as she has found that she is violently sensitive to bee sting. They cause her whole body to swell, and though the doctor has prescribed various medications, these seem to have no effect. He assures me that there is no cause for alarm.

Your most obedient servant,

Phoebe Thomas

Pontley arrived at Manner Hall a week later, tired, dirty and in a rather poor mood, as it had rained the greater part of his journey, which should have been wholly unnecessary in any case. He was met by Phoebe, who, astonished to see him drive up to the stables, hurried out to greet him.

"We had no idea you intended to visit, my lord. Have you come to see the progress of the work?" she asked anxiously.

"I have come," he muttered darkly, "to speak with Miss Forbes. Has she recovered from her indisposition?"

"Well, not completely, but . . . Oh, dear, my letter alarmed you, did it not? How careless of me to cause you anxiety. Glenna was most particular that I should say nothing which would cause you concern or to la—" Phoebe drew herself up abruptly.

"Laugh at her? If I had had any desire to do so, the muddy roads, uncomfortable inn beds and inadequate meals on my journey would have entirely discouraged me, Miss Thomas. Where is she?"

"In her room, my lord."

He frowned. "She isn't able to get about yet?"

"The swelling has diminished somewhat and the doctor is hopeful that it will be no more than a few days now before she is perfectly restored." Phoebe caught her lower lip with even white teeth and asked beseechingly, "You will not need to see her, will you? I feel sure I can answer any of your questions about the renovations or . . . or the household. Or Mr. Glover could—or Mrs. Morgan."

Pontley considered the matter gravely, then shook his head. "No, Miss Thomas, it will be necessary for me to see Miss Forbes."

"She—she really does not see anyone but me, my lord."

"I have never thought of bee sting as contagious, Miss Thomas. Tell her to expect me in half an hour, if you please. I should like to rid myself of my dirt."

As he turned away, Phoebe clasped at his arm. With downcast eyes she murmured, "It would not be right for you to see her in her bedchamber, my lord."

"Then have her await me in the Winter Parlor."

"Oh, won't you understand?" Phoebe cried exasperatedly. "Glenna is mortified to look so . . . unlike herself."

Pontley patiently removed her hand from his arm. "It won't be the first time I have seen her . . . how did you put it? . . . unlike herself. The Winter Parlor, I think, ma'am." He strode off before Phoebe could protest further, and she reluctantly made her way to her friend's room.

Glenna was alarmed by the distressed countenance Phoebe presented to her. "Whatever is the matter?"

"Lord Pontley has come. He wishes to see you in the Winter Parlor in half an hour," she gasped.

"Well, you must tell him that I am indisposed."

"I tried to do so, Glenna, but he will have none of it."

Glenna pushed aside the account books on which she had been working, rose and went to examine herself in the glass. Her face was still puffy and her hair disheveled, as it was painful for her to brush it. "He has a most awkward habit of arriving when he is least wished for. Can you make me presentable, Phoebe?"

Her friend nodded, but her efforts, however careful, were painful to Glenna, who gently thanked her and begged that she desist. Instead she dug in her dressing table drawer for a cap of white lace which she ruthlessly tied over the red-gold curls. "That will have to do. I should not like to run into Peter again. Is he out?"

"Yes, until dinner, I believe. Glenna, he . . . he was only startled and concerned when first he saw you so swollen."

"My dear girl, I do not blame him, but I cannot wish to repeat the experience," she said dryly. "I consider it a wonder, after seeing his expression, that he did not pack his bags and depart within the hour."

"That's unfair, Glenna. He has been most solicitous of your welfare—you know you laugh at his notes—and he has entertained Caroline, Ralph and me in the evenings."

"Poor Peter. It cannot have been the sort of visit he had in mind. Hopefully it will be only a short while longer before I am recovered." She picked up her account book and headed for the door.

"Do you want me to come with you?"

"No, thank you, love. I will not have Pontley think I am afraid to face him alone."

When Glenna arrived at the Winter Parlor she found her landlord leaning negligently against the window frame and she was forcefully reminded of their encounter at Lockwood. He turned to her immediately on this occasion and carefully studied the sight she presented. The swollen face and hands were the only parts of her body to be seen in her high-necked, long-sleeved gown, and the cap was totally inadequate to conceal the disordered locks. "It looks very painful, Miss Forbes."

"Truly it is not so bad as it appears, Lord Pontley. The doctor says my system is particularly slow in ridding itself of the effects, but that they should all be gone in a short time now."

"Please sit down." He drew a chair forward for her.

"Have you come to scold me, sir?"

One corner of his mouth twisted ruefully. "Yes, I suppose that was my intention, Miss Forbes, but when I find myself confronted by you looking like a rag doll someone has left out in the rain, I haven't the heart."

Glenna's eyes flared for a moment but the image he drew forth was so apposite that she could not help but grin. "You needn't restrain yourself on my account, Lord Pontley."

"Why can't you brush your hair?" he asked curiously.

"My scalp aches when I do. I had Phoebe attempt it, but even to present a tidy appearance to you I could not bear it."

"You should not have bothered." There was a note of concern in his voice but he turned directly to other matters. "Miss Forbes, why is there a deer in the stables?"

"Ah, yes, the deer. Mr. Westlake and I found him wounded in the coppice and brought him home to be tended. Phoebe says he follows her around now."

"Who follows Miss Thomas? Westlake or the deer?"

"Both of them, I should imagine. Peter is feeling rather down since I have been stuck in my room."

"I am inclined to believe it is vanity and not indisposition which keeps you there," he remarked, not unkindly.

"It is neither!" she returned sharply. "It distresses Peter to see me like this."

"Then send him on his way," he suggested callously. "The dandies always have their priorities reversed."

Glenna regarded him coldly. "Peter is not a dandy, and I do not wish to discuss him further with you. I have brought the accounts for you to review."

He waved aside the book she offered him. "I may look at them later, but if you are up to it I should like you to take me to the kitchen so that I may see for myself what all the fuss is about."

"As you wish, of course." She rose resolutely and allowed him to open the door for her, where they came face to face with Peter as he was returning from a ride. "I believe you have met Lord Pontley, Peter. He has been kind enough to come and observe the progress we are making on the renovations."

Peter bowed formally to Pontley but did not take his eyes from Glenna's face, which seemed to hold a horrid fascination for him. Pontley drew his attention by growling, "What the devil are you gawping at, Westlake?"

The younger man stiffened visibly. "Not a thing, I assure you, sir." He turned pointedly to Glenna to ask, "Shall we have the pleasure of your company at dinner today, then?"

Glenna cast a confused glance at Pontley's frozen face and nodded. "I am much better now, Peter. If you will excuse me, I should like to show Lord Pontley the kitchen."

When Peter had passed on Glenna proceeded toward the kitchen without a glance at his lordship. Through clenched teeth she said, "I am aware that this is your house, sir, but I can see no reason for you to be rude to my guest."

"It was he who was rude, Miss Forbes. No lieutenant under my command would have been so graceless."

"Can you not forget you are no longer on a quarterdeck?" Her exasperation heightened her color, and blotches appeared on her swollen cheeks. Unfortunately she happened to catch sight of herself in a glass and would have fled but for his firm hand on her arm. The grip on her tender flesh made her wince with agony and tears sprang to her eyes, but she refused to allow them to escape. "You are hurting me," she whispered in a strangled voice.

His hand was abruptly removed with an apologetic gesture. "Excuse me! I didn't think. Perhaps you should go back to your room. We can see the kitchen tomorrow."

They stood facing one another warily while Glenna recovered her equanimity. "No, I will be perfectly all right if you will refrain from touching me," she said coldly at length, and proceeded to move down the passage. As she had intended, he felt at a distinct disadvantage, a clumsy oaf who had carelessly mauled a fragile woman. His swinging gait was no longer hampered by a limp, but he refrained from catching her up, sure that he would inadvertently trip her.

Glenna provided him with a thorough tour of the small, dark kitchen, indicating what equipment and supplies were needed, and she took him outside to show him the location of the proposed new bake house. "Have you any questions?"

"Why have you taken so much trouble to earn the money to renovate the kitchen?" He stood with his hands locked behind his back, for although it felt awkward it would prevent him from performing some clumsy movement which might pain her.

"I have just spent a half hour explaining that," she responded irritably.

"You have told me why a tenant would desire such an improvement, but you have not made me understand why you have gone to such trouble."

"Oh, you sound like Peter. I did not accept your offer of a house as charity, my lord. You gave me a task to perform and I am attempting to do so to the best of my ability."

"Will you cease your wild schemes and plans if I authorize Glover to provide the funds for your kitchen?"

"It is not *my* kitchen, and Mr. Glover has been hard pressed to provide the funds he already has!" Glenna was tempted to turn her back on him and walk away, but she feared that he would forget and lay hold of her arm, so she remained rooted to the spot.

"There will be more funds with the harvest in."

"And he shall need them to purchase farm equipment! I will admit that the keeping of bees did not prove felicitous, Lord Pontley, but most of my other endeavors have turned out very well indeed, as you would see if you would bother to look at my account books." This time she did turn from him and watched horrified as he stopped his hand in mid-air from touching her. "I am not one of your sailors to be bullied and pushed around, Pontley. Even if I were not swollen from head to toe I would take objection to your continual efforts to detain me. I wonder that I did not notice it before we became engaged, for had I done, I vow I would not have agreed."

When she had taken several steps without being molested, she was nonetheless halted by the authority in his voice. "Miss Forbes, I am not finished speaking with you."

It was on the tip of her tongue to tell him that she was finished speaking with *him*, but somehow she did not do so; instead she turned to face him once more with a sigh.

"I am not used to dealing with women," he admitted grudgingly.

"Well, for the sake of your 'elf' you had best learn," she snapped.

"We will leave Miss Stafford out of our discussion, if you please, Miss Forbes."

Glenna knew she had truly discomfited him this time and, perversely, wished she had not. Stricken with a sense of guilt, she found herself unable to speak, for although he had indeed annoyed her several times this afternoon, she was aware of the patience with which he had tolerated her insistence on having her way over the renovations. There was also, she thought miserably, the fact that he had provided her with a home, and a horse, and an occupation during her time of grief.

Pontley regarded her bowed head suspiciously. It was most unlike the fiery young lady to knuckle under, and he had not meant to cow her, but her mention of Miss Stafford, in light of his thoroughly mixed emotions on that particular head, could only add to his slightly frayed nerves. "Perhaps I should tell you that, far from disapproving of some of your innovations at Manner Hall, I have instituted several similar measures at Huntley."

"No, have you?" She lifted her head and met his eyes. "Which ones?"

"Not bee keeping," he said ruefully, "but we now have a

dairy maid and a gamekeeper. The grounds could not justify a gardener as yet, and fortunately they are planned to look rather disordered. I really feel it would be wise for me to return to Lockwood to study the workings there. It is a far better-run establishment than either of the others was."

"Your aunt's doing, to give credit where it is due. Has she moved to the dower house?"

"Months ago, with no lessening in the vituperative pennings she sends me, I promise you. But I cannot wrest the reins from her at a distance; the agent and household staff still jump when she speaks, and God knows she is knowledgeable."

"Why not simply leave matters in her hands? Without the drains of her sons she will soon enough show a profit for you."

"I am not in the habit of allowing other people to assume my burdens, Miss Forbes."

"Is that why it makes you so angry that I have taken charge here?"

"No, my dear girl, it is not! I sent you here for a chance to catch your breath after your father's death, and you have not stood still long enough to enjoy yourself."

A slow smile spread over Glenna's swollen features. "You mistake the matter, Lord Pontley. I am never happy but when I am busy, and I cannot remember when last I so thoroughly relished what I was doing. It is beautiful here and challenging to make a go of my projects. Why, I have learned to ride, and to make cheese, and to plant herbs, and even a bit about the farming."

"To say nothing of bee keeping."

"*Very* little about bee keeping, except that I shall never try it again. Oh, and we have made visits to the castle and some of the most charming villages. There's quite a fascinating yarn market in Minehead and some lovely walks on the moor. So you see, I have not spent all my time slaving to repay you for your kindness," she concluded bluntly.

"You relieve my mind, Miss Forbes. Still, rather than undertaking any new endeavors, I will arrange with Glover to provide the funds for the kitchen. If need be, there may be some extra from Huntley from the harvest which could be used." He contemplated her steadily. "Would that be satisfactory?"

Glenna made an awkward, nervous gesture. "I have been very stubborn about the kitchen, my lord. You will do just as you please, of course. Perhaps you still do not see the necessity for any change there."

He cast his eyes heavenward and exclaimed, "Oh, for God's sake, woman. You have pleaded your cause with the ability of a barrister and I would not dream of presenting a tenant with that hole." He made a disgusted gesture toward the building, and his hand inadvertently struck her on the shoulder.

Although tears sprang to her eyes from the pain, she was overcome by a fit of laughter at his ludicrous expression of dismay. Pontley stood stiffly at attention, unable to say more than, "Forgive me," owing to her peals of mirth. After a moment he could not tell if the tears that crept down her cheeks were from pain or merriment, but he had the distinct impression that she was hysterical and he longed to shake her. Instead he barked, "Stop that, Miss Forbes."

When she lifted her head, the red-gold curls had almost entirely escaped from the lopsided cap and she pressed her lips together solemnly. "You are not a safe man to be around, Pontley."

He drew a handkerchief from his pocket and offered it to her, saying, "I am not usually so careless, ma'am." While she dabbed cautiously at the tear stains he rearranged the cap so that it sat straight on her head. "Perhaps you should rest until dinner."

"Rest?" Her eyes flashed angrily. "Do you think I am so poor-spirited and weak that I need to rest because I have been bumped about a bit? I am so relieved to be out of my room for a change that I have not the least intention of returning there until I retire for the night."

"Perhaps you would care to show me about the estate, in that case."

"Not in that antiquated carriage, but I will ride with you if you give me a moment to change."

"I have brought my curricle, Miss Forbes, so there is no need for you to return to your room to change." His grin mocked her. "Of course, if you are eager to display your riding ability—"

"I am, you know, but I will be content to be driven. You must see the lovely mare Mr. Glover chose for me. At first I thought perhaps she would be too high-spirited for me, but she is so well mannered that I had not the least problem. Mr. Glover has stabled one of his own horses here for Phoebe, and protests that our exercising him is to his advantage. Everyone has been all that is good to us, sir. Mrs. Morgan treats me as mistress of the house and Betsey is the most extraordinary cook. No wonder your meals here were better than those you get at Huntley, in spite of the depressing condition of the kitchen." They had arrived at the stables by this time and Glenna went first to the loose box where she had last seen the deer. "He is no longer here. Do you suppose they have released him?" Her disappointment was patent.

"I doubt it, as I saw him when I arrived," Pontley returned dryly.

John emerged from the tackle room and, on Glenna's

question, assured her that the deer had no intention of deserting them as yet. "He's followed Miss Thomas off to the parterre, ma'am. Tags along after her like a puppy and has as much mischief." John turned to the viscount. "Not that I mind having him around, my lord. Still small enough to manage, you see, but the ladies should realize that he shan't stay so forever."

A sigh escaped Glenna. "I shall not be able to face venison again in my life. Perhaps," she said with unusual humility, "you would consider having a deer park here, Lord Pontley."

"I fear not, Miss Forbes, much as I hate to disappoint you. Will you show me your mare while John attends to the curricle?"

Glenna led him to the furthest loose box where a small chestnut mare thrust out her head to be welcomed. "Is she not beautiful? The only thing is, I do not think she would carry your weight, sir." She moistened her lips nervously. "If . . . when I leave . . . you would consider allowing me to buy her from you?"

He glanced at her, surprised. "But she is yours. I had Glover buy her for you, and had no intention of keeping her here after you left."

"I could not accept a gift from you."

"She is not a gift, Miss Forbes. You have needed a horse for your activities here, and you have done far more than I ever anticipated. I owe you a good deal more than a horse, I dare say."

"Nonsense! I have done my best to fulfill the obligation you gave me. If we were not so lacking in knowledge, both of us, it would surely have been easier. But your provision of a home for me was your only share of the bargain."

"I have no intention of standing here arguing with you. The horse is yours." He turned abruptly and left her.

Glenna stroked the sleek neck fondly. "Very well then, I shall keep you, my pretty. He is a stubborn, opinionated man and deserves to be out of pocket for you." She meekly joined the viscount and allowed him to hand her, gently this time, into the curricle. There were the gardening improvements to be shown him, and the opportunity arose to introduce him to the gamekeeper, a young man whose youth startled him.

When they had driven on he remarked, "Surely that fellow cannot be above eighteen, Miss Forbes. Did Glover find him?"

"Well, no, but he was willing to take him on for a trial period, and he has proved an excellent find."

"Just where did you locate him, Miss Forbes?"

"I was told of his plight in one of the villages. His father, it seems, was a poacher who had drowned recently, leaving a large family in grave poverty." Glenna forestalled his protest by continuing, "There is nothing dishonest about young Jed. Mr. Glover has kept a careful eye on him and sings his praises. Rather than wages, we have allocated a large cottage to him and enough game to feed the family. Also, he is permitted a certain percentage of the money he receives for the game he sells. He seems more than satisfied with the arrangement and he and his brothers have put the cottage into a state of repair which can only enhance your property."

"You took a chance in hiring him."

"Only a small, calculated risk, sir. Before ever I met him I knew a great deal of his background, and that he was as unlike his father as day and night. If you have any hesitancy, you must speak with Mr. Glover."

"I am not questioning your choice, merely interested in it." Pontley turned his head to bestow a smile on her. "You are forever mocking me about seeing things in terms of a naval campaign, ma'am, but you seem to have attacked the problems at

Manner with a similar strategy which I can but admire."

Glenna was inexplicably confused by his approval, and disconcerted by his warm smile. Not often had she evoked it, with the deepening of the cleft in his chin and the lightening of his brown eyes. "Thank you. You are too generous."

Unaware that he did so, he drew the team to a halt and continued to stare at the puffy face beside him until Glenna felt most uncomfortable. She timidly touched a swollen cheek and murmured, "Is something the matter? Oh, Lord, it has become all blotchy again, hasn't it?"

"No," he assured her as he gently touched the tender flesh. "It appals me that you should suffer so in endeavoring to help me."

She sat very still as his fingers passed soothingly over her face. "It—it will be gone in a few days now, and it was through no fault of yours that I conceived such a singularly unpropitious scheme. There are any number of people in the village who keep bees. I had no way of knowing that I was sensitive to the sting."

"How did you come to be stung?" He continued to trace the curve of her cheek.

Glenna swallowed nervously. "We—we were all stung. Peter accidentally knocked over the hive. I think that is why he is so upset to see me."

Recalled by the mention of Westlake's name, Pontley removed his hand from her face, but showed no sign of unease over his action. "It is reassuring to know that he is as clumsy as I."

Somehow it was impossible to reply to him and Glenna watched bemusedly as he casually urged the horses forward. She should have rejected his touch, of course, but he had meant no harm, had in fact been excessively tender. There was no time when she was not aware of the controlled strength of him, and his concern was touching. For it *was* only concern—had he not easily returned to his horses? Was he not even now discussing estate matters as though nothing out of the ordinary had happened? He had no idea that he had done something unacceptable, she supposed, and then wondered why she should consider it unacceptable. Was there anything so wrong in his touching the swollen face? She should be grateful that he did not show any horror of her disfigurement, as Peter did. With an effort she forced herself to attend to what he was saying, and make suitable replies.

In the midst of explaining to her the plans he had for Huntley, he broke off to ask bluntly, "Why is it you call him Peter, but use my title?"

"Why . . . I don't know." He did not look at her and she clasped her hands together firmly in her lap. "I suppose it is because you have never called me Glenna."

"If I did, would you call me Philip?"

"If you wish me to, I suppose there can be nothing wrong in it, though I can see no reason for you to do so. And—and it might seem strange to the staff, you know."

"You would rather I didn't."

"I—I think it might be *best* if you didn't, though I have no objection for myself, you understand."

"Oh, yes, I understand." He made no further reference to the matter, but proceeded with his description of Huntley, apparently unmoved by the few exchanged words. When he assisted her from the curricle at the stables he merely commented, "I hope you will be joining us for dinner, Miss Forbes."

"I think I shall."

"Good. I will see you then." He strolled into the stables with a negligent wave of his hand and was soon in deep conversation with John.

NINE

Glenna made her appearance in the drawing room before dinner, which was served each day at five. The days were growing shorter and cooler and there was a welcome blaze on the hearth. This had been one of the first rooms painted and the smell still clung to it, but Glenna had as yet not seen the work, having remained for the past week and a half in self-imposed exile. She was satisfied with her inspection, as Phoebe had assured her she would be. The painted medallions on the ceiling had been cleaned and their earthy colors echoed in the faintest of tones on the walls. On the mantel the carved lyres had been made beautifully visible once again with a coat of white paint, and the Greek frieze likewise took on a crisp new character.

"Very nice," Glenna murmured. "The only problem is that the carpet and floor look so much shabbier in contrast, to say nothing of the furniture. Remind me, Phoebe . . ." She caught sight of Pontley in the doorway and ceased speaking.

He nodded to the assembled company before making a minute inspection of the room. "I had no idea it was so handsome an apartment, and I must congratulate you on your choice of colors, Miss Forbes. If every room could be so transformed . . ."

"There is no chance of that, Lord Pontley," she laughed. "This is by far the best proportioned room, though I am inclined to think the dining room will look very smart because of its tall windows. It might be best, when the house is shown to prospective tenants, to remove the draperies there altogether. That may cause some consternation, because of a tenant realizing that he will need to provide them himself, but it must be better than ruining the effect with those sun-bleached, tattered rags."

"I take it you think the draperies should be replaced."

"Well, of course they should, but I am not going to do battle with you on that head, I promise you."

Peter could not resist interpolating. "You have done more than enough, Glenna. I am persuaded Lord Pontley had no intention of your working day and night to restore his house." He threw a belligerent glance at the viscount.

"None whatsoever," Pontley countered genially. "I believe Miss Forbes and I have come to an agreement on that score whereby she will see those items she feels essential taken care of without further projects on her part."

"I should hope so," Peter murmured.

Glenna turned laughing eyes to Phoebe. "You must tell Lord Pontley, my dear, how I have worked my fingers to the bone, and ruined my eyesight reading late into the night one of those dusty books from the library. Dull stuff, that, with not a moment's leisure for trips and excursions. Why, when Captain Andrews came I had to lock myself in the library to keep from being dragged away to see some wretched castle, and only allowed myself to be persuaded in order to offer you chaperonage."

Phoebe, entering into the spirit of the discussion, proclaimed, "And not a moment to spare for a walk on the beaches at Minehead or the lonely paths on the moors. How have you borne it, Glenna? No time to play the harp or ride your little mare or entertain your friends." She waved an encouraging hand to the Carmichaels, who were also still in residence, and they assisted her with a list of activities in which they had participated.

Under this onslaught Peter looked uncomfortable for his championing of Glenna, but Pontley's lips twitched ruefully. "We are agreed, then, that Miss Forbes has found time to enjoy herself in spite of her hardships. I hope she will continue to do so." Dinner was announced and, to Peter's chagrin, Pontley offered his arm to Glenna, and was not rebuffed. It was only natural under the circumstances but still he chafed under Pontley's behavior, which seemed to him autocratic and callous. Peter was well aware that his own manners were more polished, his address more refined than the viscount's would ever be. There was a roughness about his manner not only in the features, but in his actions, which Peter condemned from his own viewpoint of social elegance. It was a Westlake tradition to attend to the niceties of behavior and he gallantly escorted Phoebe into the yet unpainted dining room.

Now here Peter knew he excelled. His conversation was amusing and his knowledge of London society vast. Fortunately he received a steady stream of letters which kept him current with the latest gossip, and since Glenna had been absent for so long, he regaled the company with stories he felt they would enjoy. The facility with which he wove a tale was every bit as clever as the notes he had fired off to Glenna during her illness, and he was rewarded by seeing her laugh frequently. He could not be entirely comfortable with her puffy features, and rather wished that she had not emerged so soon from her retirement, but he was aware that the condition was temporary, and largely his fault.

"And I have at last discovered why the younger Stafford girl did not make her come-out this spring," he declared triumphantly, unaware of the stiffening of Pontley's face or the anxious glance Glenna cast at him. "They say she is a very highly strung girl and that her parents felt a sojourn with her sister in the country would be beneficial, but from what Carstairs wrote, *I* think—"

"Peter," Glenna interrupted firmly, "you are forgetting that Lord Pontley's aunt is related to this young lady. I had much rather hear what your mother has to say of the imminent arrival of King Louis's brother and whether there will be a reconciliation between the Prince of Wales and his father."

Since Glenna had very little interest in either of these topics, and Peter was momentarily struck dumb, Phoebe turned to Pontley to fill the breach. "I must tell you how much we enjoyed our trip on board Captain Andrews's ship, my lord. We had delightful weather, except for one storm, and found the experience quite exhilarating. Captain Andrews was everything that was kind and has been so thoughtful as to call on us to see how we go on."

"I had heard from him that the passage went well, and that he found the company of two young ladies most welcome." He did not miss the faint blush which arose on Phoebe's cheeks, and turned to Glenna. "It is not often he is provided with concerts on board ship, ma'am, and he expressed an uncommon appreciation of your playing of the harp. I had thought perhaps you would swathe it in rags and oilcloth to preserve it from the elements."

"I had intended to, but Phoebe cannot restrain pinching at me about it ever since I stuffed it in the chaise to take to the vicarage. No damage resulted from the sea breezes."

"Perhaps you would honor me with a performance this evening."

The request, however natural, took on added significance when his eyes held Glenna's so intently. It occurred to her that he might be mocking her, for she had not forgotten the occasion on which she informed him that she was aware that her playing was one of the reasons he had offered for her. "I should like to oblige, sir, but my hands are still too swollen to do so with comfort."

"Of course. Another time."

Peter had by now recovered his equanimity and was not content to remain a bystander to the conversation. He was just as glad that Glenna would not be playing, as he had no real interest in music, though he was proud of her accomplishment and willing to reflect in her glory from it. With the dexterity of years of social practice, he unobtrusively regained the attention of his audience and began once more to lead the conversation gracefully into topics on which he was by far the most knowledgeable person in the room.

After dinner, while the Carmichaels walked in the garden, the other four played a few desultory hands of whist, but Glenna could see that Pontley's casual game did not mesh with Peter's avid involvement in his cards, and she suggested that she might show the viscount about the house to enumerate her plans for the color scheme of each room. Phoebe caught the look of annoyance in Peter's eyes and challenged him to a game of cribbage, to which he reluctantly acquiesced.

Glenna's obvious enthusiasm for her projects amused Pontley, but it also forced him to compare the mature decision with which she attacked them to the childlike, unsubstantial eagerness of Miss Stafford. There was a fairylike fragility about the latter which begged for a man's protectiveness, but Pontley could not look on Glenna's puffed countenance without a twinge of—what? He refused to delve more deeply into his reaction.

"I thought the library should be painted a soothing color," Glenna was explaining, "and yet the books are so dark and heavy, don't you think? So I have chosen a cream, with a darker trim to emphasize its lightness and yet harmonize with the volumes. Does that seem a good idea?" She glanced up at him as he stood holding the branch of candles, his eyes again fixed on her face in such a way that she drew a sharp breath.

Before she could fully realize his intention, he had set the candles absently on the desk and, holding her shoulders gently, bent to kiss her. Glenna made no attempt to withdraw from him, but neither did she respond, though it was with an effort. "You . . . you must not do that. It is most improper to go about kissing young ladies," she gasped, her color heightened.

"Yes, I imagined it would be," he replied gravely, "and I have no doubt your friend Peter would strenuously object." He drew his fingers gently over her face, as he had earlier in the day.

"It is I who object. You have no right to kiss me."

"No, but I once had and did not take advantage of the opportunity. I had a desire to rectify that mistake." When she did not speak he added, "Now your face has become blotchy again."

Glenna's hands flew to her cheeks and she turned away from him. "Why are you tormenting me? What have I done to lead you to believe I will tolerate your wretched behavior?"

"Nothing, I promise you, Glenna. You must consider it a momentary aberration and forgive me if you will." In spite of his words, there was no note of apology in his voice, and he casually retrieved the branch of candles. "Your plans for this room sound well enough. Shall you show me the bedrooms next?"

Now she was sure he was mocking her, and along with a flash of anger she was overcome by a hysterical desire to giggle. In a choked voice she replied, "I shall show you nothing more, Pontley. Go away and leave me alone."

"Very well. Look at me, Glenna." He waited until she hesitantly faced him. "I am leaving for Lockwood in the morning and will not see you before I depart. Rest assured I am pleased with the progress of the renovations here, and sincerely thank you for your efforts. From now on I wish you will not work so hard but enjoy yourself as I had intended. The funds for the kitchen will be arranged so that that work may be done, and I hope you will see that additional windows are let into the existing structure there. No one should have to labor in such a hole."

"When the work is finished . . . will you come to inspect it?"

Pontley considered her for a moment. "No, I think not. Glover should have little difficulty finding a tenant. You are not to leave until you are ready, even after the renovations are completed; stay for a few months to partake of the fruits of your labor."

"When my commission is complete I shall have no cause, or desire, to stay."

"Where will you go?"

"I think it cannot be of concern to you."

"In other words, you don't know."

Glenna sighed exasperatedly. "That is not precisely what it means. I have not as yet decided whether to return to Hastings, but I suppose I shall." She had led him from the room and now stood before the drawing room. "Is my face still . . . discolored?"

Holding the candles closer, he inspected the puffy cheeks, and touched her lips with a finger. "No. Excuse me to your friends, if you will. I will bid you good night and farewell."

She nodded mutely as she slipped through the door he held open for her.

In spite of the fact that Glenna entered the events of the

day in her journal to rid her mind of them, she did not sleep well that night, and awoke to find that Lord Pontley had indeed already left. Although she told herself that she should be relieved, she could detect nothing of that feeling about herself. Instead her nerves were on edge, and much as she tried to attribute it to the fact that her face was still swollen, she was not so easily deceived. Her reflection in the glass was little better than the previous day, but this time she struggled to bring the curls under control, no matter how painful the process.

How could he have wished to kiss her when she looked so ugly? It must have been pity, she realized suddenly, and her face colored with shame. Oh, how loathesome to be an object of pity! His pity! Why, Peter could dance circles around him for grace and charm, for manners and entree into the *haut ton*. And though Peter was distressed by her appearance now, his loyalty to her could not be doubted. Just last night as she had left the room for bed he had pressed her hand and informed her, in a very meaningful way, too, that he was delighted to have her company again. It was not Peter who had wandered off and been smitten by the first pretty face he saw. Peter, Glenna informed her reflection in the mirror, had spent years among young ladies of the first stare, and he had come back to her when the obstacle to their happiness had vanished.

To be sure, Peter had not been constant in the years between, but Glenna could not have wished him to be. As the pain of their parting had lessened, she had grown to expect that he would marry elsewhere, and had been almost surprised each time a letter had come from Lady Garth when it did not contain that intelligence. It had amused Glenna that Lady Garth continued the correspondence, almost as though the older woman had forgotten its original purpose and slid into the habit of exchanging letters, so intent was she on spreading word of any unusual happening in London. Her letters now acknowledged Peter's renewed interest and she hastened to assure Glenna that memory was short amongst her circle, and that Glenna had not, she hoped, taken too seriously her previous reports of Peter's flirts. Well, they had come to nothing, after all, had they? Lady Garth pointed out, commenting rather caustically that it was high time Peter settled down. Surely Glenna had not the least need of Pontley's pity, and she would have been glad to tell him so—in fact, ached to do so.

In an excess of emotion she tugged unmercifully at her hair and refused to stop until she had it completely under control, although her eyes teared and her scalp smarted with the abuse. Satisfied, she donned another high-necked, long-sleeved gown of gray wool and marched determinedly to the breakfast table. Today she would begin organizing the work for the kitchen. The sooner she could shake the dust of Manner Hall from her, the better.

Peter, now accustomed to her unnatural features, greeted her cheerfully with the news that the lord of the manor had taken himself off as abruptly as he had arrived.

"Yes, and I am glad of it," Glenna grumbled. "He does nothing but bully when he is around one."

Struck with the similarity to his own thoughts, Peter decreed, "Too autocratic by half, he is, my dear, and without the least pretense of understanding a lady's finer feelings."

"Certainly not!" she agreed, her face flushing slightly.

"I wonder that you should have been engaged to him at one time."

"I did not know him so well then," she returned sadly.

"Ah, well, you have learned better, and have had a lucky escape."

Glenna made no response, as she was intent on spreading

her toast with butter. Convinced that it would be best to change the subject, she did so. "Would you care to ride in to Minehead with me this morning, Peter? I have several commissions to undertake."

"No doubt for the landlubber land lord," Peter quipped, pleased with his wit.

"You are a guest in his house, Peter."

Quelled by her frown, he mumbled an apology, such as it was, and agreed that he would ride with her. When Phoebe entered the breakfast room, Peter reestablished himself by chatting with her so that Glenna had an opportunity to plan what she wanted to accomplish in town. It was not really difficult to allow his words to drift past her and concentrate on other matters.

TEN

Pontley had only been driving for two hours, and was looking to his first change in Taunton when he overtook a cavalcade of impressive proportions. First he passed the inferior stablemen, the hack-horses, the whipper-in, and the pack of hounds; next the hunters with cloths of scarlet trimmed with silver, attended by the stud-groom and huntsman; at length a chaise marine with four horses carrying numerous services of plate escorted by several household members with blunderbusses. But the procession was headed by no less than three other vehicles: a coach and six with two postillions, coachman and three outriders; a post chaise and four post horses; plus a phaeton and four followed by two grooms. The upper servants rode in the coach while the mistress of the establishment luxuriated in the chariot. But the master, Pontley was told in Taunton when he described the remarkable procession, traveled only in the phaeton, and in all weathers, wrapped in his swan's-down coat. Pontley would have thought no more of it, other than perhaps that it seemed the sort of ostentation in which Miss Stafford would revel, had he not happened to catch the owner's name.

The shock of learning that it was indeed Miss Stafford's parents, Sir George and Lady Stafford, headed from their estate in Cornwall to another in Leicestershire, was enough to give him pause. He had not been informed that Miss Stafford's parents were due to arrive at Lord and Lady Morris's, yet such an expedition must have been planned for some time, and it was but a few days since he had left Huntley. On the other hand he found it difficult to believe that they would not visit their daughters on their journey northward. Pontley had, it was true, left the Huntley estate rather precipitously when he learned of Miss Forbes's accident with the bees, and he had intended to return there after he evaluated the situation at Manner Hall.

All in all, he did not like the disposition of the forces ranging against him, and he had no intention of bowing to the pressures brought to bear on him. Miss Stafford's sister, Lady Morris, had become a little less circumspect in her hints that an offer from him was expected. Pontley's Aunt Gertrude wrote in her usual impatient vein urging him to get on with it. And now this. He had a brief thought to drive on and affect never having realized who the travelers were, but it appeared cowardly to him, and it was his nature to face disagreeable tasks head on. Reluctantly he asked the ostler to inform Sir George Stafford that Lord Pontley would await him in a private parlor if he would be so kind as to step into the inn.

Not only Sir George but his wife joined Pontley there. The viscount could detect no resemblance to Jennifer Stafford in her gruff, red-faced father, but Lady Stafford, for all her more than forty years, had an ethereal quality and delicate features much like her daughter. It was appalling to Pontley to see this older version of the girl, for, as he had suspected, the childlike quality did not become the woman—made her, rather, appear ridiculous with her hair dressed as an ingenue and her driving costume too revealing to be flattering on a woman whose body had not stood the years. Not that her appearance was of paramount importance; it was the inability to deal with reality which alarmed him.

"Well, well, well, so you are Lord Pontley. We've heard a great deal about you, a great deal," Sir George blustered, his eyes taking in the young man in great detail. "My wife, your lordship, Lady Stafford."

A whimsical smile flitted about Lady Stafford's lips. "*Delighted* to make your acquaintance, Lord Pontley. We had been looking forward to meeting you when we arrived at Cromer Lodge. Such a coincidence that we should meet on the road!"

"Yes, indeed. Do you intend to stay long at the lodge?" he asked politely.

She cast an uncertain glance at her husband, and he stepped in. "Really can't say as yet. Haven't seen our daughters in some months and you know how it is when the ladies get talking. Hard to prise them apart."

"I had intended to return to Huntley after my visit to Manner Hall, but my plans are changed and I am now headed for Lockwood. When I learned that it was you I had passed on the road, I could not miss the opportunity to make your acquaintance. Lady Morris and Miss Stafford speak of you frequently."

Sir George grunted at this intelligence and Lady Stafford fluttered about, expressing concern. "We had so hoped to have the opportunity to get to know you, my lord. It was our understanding that you frequently visit Cromer."

"Lord and Lady Morris have been very tolerant of my presence, and have been most helpful in introducing me to the neighborhood. Miss Stafford, too, has afforded me her company on rides and drives to various spots of interest. She appears to relish the country life and her enthusiasm is contagious."

Dissatisfied with the casual way in which this information was delivered, Sir George pressed on. "Engaging little puss, our Jennifer. Has the looks of her mother, too, thank heaven. Deeply attached to her, we are. Not to say we would hold her back from an eligible match—no, no, just the thing for her. Needs a bit of a guiding hand."

Pontley was strongly tempted to inform Sir George that in his opinion Miss Stafford was in need of a keeper, not a husband, but he of course refrained. Instead he chose his words carefully. "Miss Stafford is still young to undertake the responsibilities of marriage. I should hate to see her burdened with the management of some household when her chief delight is roaming about her brother-in-law's property knowing the carefree life of a child."

"No, no," Lady Stafford almost squeaked. "Why, Jennifer is eighteen and looks forward to a household of her own. Would not any young lady? I was married at eighteen and found it the greatest comfort to have an establishment of my own. I have often told you so, have I not, Sir George?"

"Yes, m'dear, so you have. 'Twill be the making of the girl, you know," he informed Pontley. "Needs a little responsibility to settle her, don't you see?"

The viscount refused to falsely agree to this piece of nonsense. Nothing and nobody was going to "settle" Miss Stafford, as unfortunate as the matter was. She was a charming, delightful child, but with swings of mood so violent as to astonish an observer. On his first visit Pontley had seen only the affectionate, joyous vitality of the girl. When he had ridden up to Cromer Lodge on his return he had witnessed another side altogether. Thwarted in her desire to rid herself of the tiny groom who perpetually followed her about, Pontley had watched horrified as she viciously struck the little lad, causing him to fall from his mount. Miss Stafford had been unaware of Pontley's presence, but on seeing him she had rushed to assure him that the groom had attempted to take liberties with her. The episode had been followed, if not by such a drastic example, at least by unnerving ones, which had disillusioned him, in spite of the infectiousness of her personality when she was "herself." He had attempted to understand her, to help her to achieve some moderation of her black moods and violent temper, but with no noticeable results.

Recalled to the present from these meditations by Lady Stafford's rambling monologue on her daughter's virtues, Pontley politely agreed that the girl was charming. "I should not delay your journey longer, ma'am. If your stay at Cromer is lengthy, no doubt we will meet there. I hope you will convey my regards to your daughters and Lord Morris." With a leisurely bow and a forced amiability, he took leave of the disgruntled couple, aware that he had not performed the only civility which would have been acceptable to them—to have offered for Miss Stafford.

The rest of his journey was uncomfortable. The roads were tolerable, the posting inns acceptable, the meals edible, but he could not rid himself of his nagging thoughts of Miss Stafford. It was permissible, by his lights, to extricate himself from her sister's hints and her parents' encouragement; they were plots, rather too obvious ones, to entrap him into marrying the girl. He could not so easily abandon the girl herself. His original infatuation had disintegrated, but it had been replaced by a brotherly concern which had led him to attempt to help her. He was aware that his attentions to the girl had raised unholy hopes in her sister's breast, which she had obviously shared with her parents. Pontley could easily discount their predatory claims on him; they were all intent on thrusting the girl onto someone else's shoulders. She was a responsibility none of them bore gladly. Selfishly intent on their own pleasures, she symbolized for each a chain which bound them.

Even that Pontley could have walked away from, uneasily.

But the girl's devotion to him was another matter entirely. He had been flattered by her admiration of him when they first met; it was very different, after all, from Miss Forbes's unemotional acceptance of him as a prospective husband—and one whom she had wished at sea for the greater part of the time. Pontley had, by his actions, led Miss Stafford to believe that he was attached to her but that his engagement bound him to another. When the engagement was broken she had every right to expect that he would offer for her.

Unfortunately, he had lost the desire to do so when he had seen her erratic and often violent behavior, but his sense of responsibility, as with Miss Forbes, had prompted him not to abandon her. His efforts to teach her to control her temper were unavailing; his attempts to lift her from black moods unprofitable. But his attentions to her had strengthened her affection for him, apparently, and no amount of discussion, perhaps too delicately put (Peter Westlake would have been astonished), could convince the girl that her feelings were not reciprocated in quite the same way. It was incomprehensible to her that he should feel differently than she did herself; that he should not wish to marry her and take her away from the unfeeling people around her. And although Pontley recognized her genuine affection for him, he was not convinced as she seemed to be that it was a deep and abiding love. In her unconscious selfishness she clung to the one person who showed an interest in her.

Pontley's arrival at Lockwood did not relieve him of these thoughts, and his aunt summoned him to the dower house almost before he had time to change. Irritated with the imperiousness of the message, he sent word that he would wait on her the following morning and hoped she was in good health. There were matters to be attended to on the estate, and his leg had begun to ache with fatigue. He was in no mood to sustain her bitter recriminations.

Owing to the experience he had gained at Huntley and Manner, he was able to discuss matters more intelligently with the Lockwood agent. Since there had been no more heavy drains on the estate since his cousin had died, affairs were prospering and Pontley reminded himself to thank his aunt for her overseeing of the estate. It was high time he settled there and involved himself with its management.

At dinner he gazed out the window over the manicured lawns to the distant gentle hills and for the first time experienced a real feeling for the place. He could not, in this room, deny those thoughts of Miss Forbes which he had forced from him since he left Manner. It was uselessly idle to reflect on the meal they had shared here at Lockwood, or to dwell on the emotion which had seized him a few days previously. He drained the brandy glass, set it down with a sharp clink and rose to pace across to the windows. She was intent on having her first love, the exquisitely dressed Mr. Westlake, and there was nothing he could do about it. Her choice, he thought, was a poor one, and he would not have expected it of her, with her calm capability, her mature vitality, her ridiculous puffy cheeks. He turned away from the view he was no longer regarding and made his way to the stables.

"I have had a most distressing letter from Jennifer this morning," Lady Pontley informed him the moment he entered her sitting room.

"Have you indeed? Is something amiss with Miss Stafford?"

"Her parents had just arrived and informed her that they met you en route. Jennifer was shocked that you did not intend to return to Huntley as you had promised her." Her cold eyes raked him, to no avail.

"I should not have called it a promise, Aunt Gertrude, and I have written to inform Lord Morris of my intention to spend some time at Lockwood. There are matters here which I should attend to."

"You are not equipped to take care of anything here, as I should think you would know by now, and did better to leave matters in my hands."

"Nonetheless, I do not intend to, though I thank you most sincerely for your continued interest in the estate. Smitt will be showing me about in an hour's time. I take it there is some problem with the winter wheat in the north field."

The dowager pointed a bony finger at him which shook with her agitation. "You are acting dishonorably, Pontley."

A muscle twitched at the corner of his firmly closed mouth, but he stretched his aching leg before answering her. "I am not aware of it, ma'am. Perhaps you would be so kind as to explain."

"You have led my poor niece to believe that you intend to marry her, yet my brother writes that you gave no such assurance to him. He believes that you have been trifling with the girl's affections, and Lady Stafford is so overwrought that they find they cannot continue their journey to Leicestershire."

A vision of the procession he had encountered on the road to Taunton arose in Pontley's mind and he could not blame Lady Stafford for shrinking from shepherding such an assemblage, but he would not evade the issue. "When I was interested in marrying your niece, I was previously engaged, my dear aunt. By the time I was free from my betrothal, I had learned that I no longer wished to do so. I have spoken with Miss Stafford concerning my feelings on the subject, but she is not able to comprehend my meaning."

"My niece is not half-witted, Pontley. You have been a

constant visitor at Cromer and in frequent attendance upon her. Lady Morris assures me that your attentions have been most particular to the girl and she is at a loss to understand why you have not come up to scratch."

"Let us be frank, Aunt. Miss Jennifer Stafford is a charming, bright and very beautiful young lady. She is also unbalanced. Her father may say that she needs a firm hand to guide her, her mother that she needs the responsibilities of matrimony, and her sister that she is an ingenuous sprite, but the truth of the matter is that she is disturbed. Her temper is uncontrollable; I should know, I have tried. She changes in an instant from the heights of alt to the deepest depression. These are not matters which encourage me to offer for her."

"How dare you accuse my niece of being mentally unstable? She is little more than a child, though perhaps a trifle wild. I cautioned my brother years ago that he should not allow her the freedom he did, but I was not heeded, of course." Her glare did not discompose him, but her next words were more successful. "In any case, you have led the girl to believe that you would marry her, and you are bound to act on your honor."

"I have given considerable thought to the matter, Aunt Gertrude. Had I been dealing with a normal woman, I would not find myself in this hobble. Miss Stafford, however, refuses to acknowledge what I have explained to her several times, which is that I should like to be her friend, but not her husband. I have endeavored to make a change in her behavior, to find whether she can maintain a certain stability, but the effort was wasted."

"You will have more control as her husband, Pontley. The child writes desperately of her attachment to you, of your promises to her. No gentleman would trifle with a child's affections as you have done."

"The problem is, my dear aunt, that she is a child and is like to remain a child, no matter what her age. Her mother has only a limited grasp on reality, I should say from my short acquaintance with her; Miss Stafford has essentially none. She does precisely what she wishes, when she wishes, and if she is crossed flies into a rage. It is unfortunate that I did not have the opportunity to observe her for longer when I was first at Huntley."

"Unfortunate, yes, but irremediable now, Pontley. You must marry the girl." His aunt, who had sneered at his honor where Miss Forbes was involved, was prepared now to use it to her advantage. After all, this was her niece, and, from his description, a young lady enough like her widgeon mother that Lady Pontley did not doubt she would be able to bring Jennifer under her control with a minimum of effort. She had had some inkling that there was more to Jennifer's story than the tale of being high strung, but it made little difference to her. Lady Pontley envisaged a chance to retain some influence at Lockwood through her niece. Her lips curled sardonically and her voice grated as she proclaimed, "I shall invite her to visit me, and you may offer for her while she is here. You have no choice, Pontley. In her letter she has resorted to the wildest accusations, and who can blame her in her heartbroken state? A few such letters would damage your reputation beyond repair, and surely you, knowing her as you do, cannot believe that she would be inhibited from sending them far and wide."

He should have known that Miss Stafford would not be able to handle his apparent rejection in not returning to Huntley, but he had not really thought of that angle. With a sigh he acquiesced to his aunt's plan; he would probably have felt it necessary to marry the child in any case. He would have to make the best of it, married to an unruly child who could be entertaining as well as exasperating, but he was aware that he was not a particularly patient man. In many ways he had tried to spare her as well as himself, for he knew he would not make her a comfortable husband. She ought to have someone indulgent, who would be amused by her flights of fancy and tolerant of her fitful moods. Although Pontley wished the girl well, he was too practical a man to deceive himself that he would be happy with her. She would be a constant burden and a source of pain, but he would do his best to see that she did not suffer for his unwillingness.

"Very well, have her come to you, aunt. She should have an opportunity to become familiar with Lockwood." Her smug satisfaction piqued him, and he added coldly, "No doubt you will appreciate the opportunity to become re-acquainted with her. Miss Stafford informed me that she had not seen you since she was ten. I should warn you, perhaps, that she is fond of dressing up as a boy." With this parting shot, he bowed and headed for the door.

"She will not do so in *my* house," the old woman retorted.

Pontley merely smiled at her.

ELEVEN

As November progressed Glenna had the satisfaction of watching the kitchen change from a depressing hole into a useful modern area. Betsey managed throughout the work to provide her usual standard of fare, and Mrs. Morgan wept when she saw the new range.

As soon as Glenna's ordinary countenance reappeared, Peter began to press his suit. "I know it is not six months since your father died, my dear, but I am sure he would have been delighted to see you married. There is no need, I am persuaded, to wait until you are out of black gloves."

"No, of course not, but we are only now getting to know one another again, Peter."

"It did not take you so long to decide the first time," he laughed.

"We were so young then. I have changed, you know, and am become very set in my ways." Glenna reluctantly closed the account books she had been studying and attempted to give him her whole attention.

"Pooh! You have been hibernating. Just wait until you are in London, my love. There is nothing in Hastings, and certainly not *here*, to hold you for a moment. No assemblies or routs, no card parties or musical evenings. I wonder you can bear it. And you shall play the harp for our friends. Do you not remember how impressed all of London was with your playing?"

"Yes, my dear, but I was a sort of prodigy then because of

my youth, a claim which hardly holds true now," she replied dryly. "And I do not know anyone in London."

"Well, you will like my friends," he said dubiously. "At least, young Spears married last August and his wife is very elegant. I have heaps of cousins, too—young ladies who would be delighted to show you about. My sister Julia is on the verge of marrying and I think they plan to establish in the city. I should hope so, since his seat is somewhere in Scotland or Ireland or some such place. So you see, there will be plenty of people for you to go about with."

"I take it you had no intention of hanging about me yourself?"

Peter looked truly appalled. "It's hardly the thing, Glenna. I mean, of course I would be about and escort you occasionally to the theatre or the opera. But you would be invited to join other parties when I was off at Brooks's or . . . somewhere or other."

"I see. Peter, do you really wish to marry?" she asked curiously.

He drew himself up stiffly as though his word had been impugned. "Why ever would you ask such a question? Have I not been begging you to marry me? Offering you inducements to do so?"

"Were those inducements?" she asked faintly.

"Well, of course they are! Are you not forever prosing on about being too independent to marry? I am showing you that it is possible to go your own way after you are hitched. We would have a very comfortable arrangement. My father has settled a neat little property on me, and my godfather, bless his soul, made it possible for me to enjoy all the elegancies of life. There will be no need for you to pinch pennies, as you have all your life, I don't doubt. I enjoy gambling but I never lose my head over it, so you needn't fear we would land in the basket on that score."

"I am relieved to hear it." Her eyes danced with laughter, but he waved aside such levity.

"I am serious, Glenna. There is something more, too." He appeared to hesitate, and rose to pace about the room so that he need not meet her inquiring eyes. "I would not keep you forever breeding, as my older brothers do their wives. Why, those poor ladies have hardly had a chance to wear clothes with some shape since they married. I should like an heir, of course, but I have no real interest in having a parcel of brats about, forever throwing up on my coats and tugging my pantaloons out of shape. You should see Roger after he's spent an hour with his brood! Well, never mind, but I thought you might like to know," he finished lamely.

Glenna was hard pressed not to laugh; the vision of Peter staring horror-stricken at a befouled coat was strong indeed. "I—I appreciate your consideration, Peter."

"There, now," he sighed, "I know it is not a proper matter to raise but I thought I should just tell you how I felt."

"I am glad you did."

"And will you marry me, Glenna?"

"I should like a few days to think on it, please, Peter. You have been very kind to be so open with me, and I assure you that I have a better idea now of what you offer me. My own recommendations are few, as you know. It surprises me that your family would be willing to condone such an alliance."

"Nonsense. My mother is fond of you, and she has always had a special soft spot for me, don't you know. I should like to take you home with me, and I must be leaving in a few days. Mother enclosed an invitation for you in the letter I received today." He patted his pockets and finally withdrew the appropriate item. "Here, see for yourself. It would give you a chance to meet the whole of the family, for everyone comes to the castle for Christmas."

Glenna received the gilded sheet from him and, from years of experience, quickly deciphered the scratchings thereon. Lady Garth indeed extended her hospitality and had no doubt that there would be good tidings brought with the young couple. Glenna sighed and slipped the letter into the desk drawer. "You shall have an answer in three days, Peter."

With a shrug he accepted this as the best he could do for the moment, but he made sure, during his allotted time, that he rode frequently with her. On these occasions he was witty and complimentary, and he even attempted once to kiss her. He was not particularly successful, but it was his own fault, as he chose to execute this feat when they were both astride nervously prancing horses, and he did not repeat the attempt.

On the day Glenna was to answer him Phoebe burst into her room while she was still sipping her chocolate in bed, one of the few luxuries she allowed herself. Phoebe plumped herself down on the counterpane and said provocatively, "You will never guess what Mama sent me."

"No, I dare say I won't, goose. Give me a hint."

"Well, it is an item from the London paper."

"And of concern to you?"

"Not to me, precisely, but I thought it would be of interest to you."

Glenna felt a shiver go through her. "An announcement of Lord Pontley's engagement to Miss Stafford?" she hazarded, determinedly keeping her face neutral.

"I can see I gave you too good a hint," Phoebe pouted. "Here, you can read it for yourself. He hasn't written you, has he?"

"No, I have not heard from him since he left. There was no need to communicate with him when the work was progressing so well. I had intended to write when it was complete." She scanned the brief announcement and returned it to her friend. "I shall write to congratulate him, of course, and send your good wishes."

"Yes, do, for no matter how gruff he is I cannot help but like him. Will it change your situation here?"

"Oh, no. I intend to leave when the renovation is complete, though he said I need not hurry away. Does your family want you home for Christmas?"

"I have been meaning to speak with you about that. Papa insists that I come and bring you . . . unless you have other plans." She regarded Glenna closely, but her friend made no attempt to reply. "Will you be ready to leave in a few weeks?"

"The kitchen is very nearly finished now."

"Papa hopes you will stay with us until you decide what you wish to do. Would that please you, love?"

Glenna forced herself to smile. "You know I am fond of staying at the vicarage, and I could have no more congenial companion than you, but . . . Phoebe, I have some things I must do. Could we discuss this more later?"

"Of course." Phoebe rose immediately and pressed her friend's hand. "There is a saying about marrying in haste and repenting at leisure. I want you only to be happy, my dear."

"I know you do, and I appreciate your thought." Glenna had a strong desire to cling to her friend and pour out her indecision and her sadness, but she restrained the impulse. "Run along now, so I can get dressed." Left alone Glenna pushed back the bedclothes and automatically climbed out of bed and began to don the dress Alice had pressed and left out for her. There should have been no surprise in the announcement, and no reaction to it. Had she not known all along that he intended to wed the elfin Miss Stafford? A momentary aberration, he had called his kiss, and she had been so stupid as to think of it more often than she would admit. Even a kiss out of pity had moved her more than ten thousand of Peter's words (and he seemed to speak that many each day). And Peter's kiss—pooh, hardly that even. An apologetic attempt to make her believe that he wished to marry her because he loved her. She did not believe it. What she did believe was that he had arrived at a time of his life when it seemed convenient to have a wife and his sentimental nature had been assuaged by their earlier attachment and her release at just that time from any obstacles which might hinder her from accepting him.

Glenna felt no betrayal of her father in considering Peter's offer. Her father could no longer be hurt by such worldly concerns, and surely his only desire for her was that she be happy. But would she be with Peter? He offered her the security of worldly goods and asked little in exchange. There was no denying that he was an amiable young man, but he had no real interest other than amusing himself. He had not been trained for a political or diplomatic career or for the management of his estate, or for the military. Glenna was perplexed when she tried to envision how he spent his days in London. More to the point, she could not imagine how she would spend hers. In Hastings she had assisted her father with his research into the history of the coastal towns of Kent and Sussex, and turned his notes over to the University when he died, as he had instructed.

London, for all its amusements, appeared a desert to her. She had entered into the challenge of renovating Manner Hall with an enthusiasm she could not sustain, she was sure, through hours of card parties and morning calls. The society in which Peter lived and breathed held only the smallest of fascinations for her. As an eighteen-year-old she had been overawed by meeting the members of the *ton*, putting faces to the names she had read in the papers. Heady stuff for one so young. But now? She was not amused by the bizarre lives of the *ton*, the gambling mania and the indiscreet liaisons. Oh, Peter could make it sound wickedly fun with his turn of a phrase, his comically lifted eyebrows. He did not condemn or approve, but saw the ridiculous and turned it into an anecdote. Belonging as he did to that sphere, he accepted the actions of others as a matter of course, and no doubt indulged as thoughtlessly as they.

She chided herself for her unusually harsh viewpoint. There were many, Peter among them, who contributed generously to charities. If she married him she might take an interest in such activities, and she doubted he would disapprove. His attitude toward children she might have guessed, and she had no more desire than the next woman to prove a brood mare. Peter would be considerate; it would be a matter of pride with him.

Her toilette completed, she descended to the breakfast parlor, where Phoebe and Peter were already established. The Carmichaels, even in the country, seldom rose before eleven. Peter smiled warmly and Glenna took the opportunity, when he spoke to Phoebe, to study him. His sandy hair was as usual carefully arranged in the current wind-swept fashion. His clothes were perhaps too formal for the country but fit him to admiration, and though his frame was not large, he was well built. She supposed he could be called handsome, but his face was too regular and his eyes too mild to spell a strongly masculine countenance. On the dance floor he excelled, with the grace of an artist, and he was an elegant if not a bruising rider.

When Phoebe excused herself, Peter turned to his hostess

and took her hand in an eager clasp. "Well, love, will you have me?"

It was on the tip of her tongue to say yes. Married to him, she would no longer have financial worries, or need to make a decision as to what she should do with her life. There was no course so acceptable to a young woman as marriage, and he would provide a considerate if unexciting husband. Pontley was marrying his "elf," and she would not see him again. But her very being rebelled and she answered softly, "No, Peter, I cannot marry you, much as I like you. You have a way of life which would not suit me, I fear, and I would be a weight to you and an oddity in your circle."

His face dropped lamentably, and for a moment Glenna wondered if she had done the right thing. When he spoke she was reassured. "Nonsense, Glenna. You would come to delight in the London scene. There would be no need for you to expend your efforts on projects like this." He gave a careless wave about him. "Instead you would have only to amuse yourself. Your leisure time would be total."

Glenna could not repress a chuckle. "I cannot bear the thought of it, Peter. Pray say no more. I am truly grateful for your kindness and your . . . loyalty to me, but I cannot marry you."

Confused and a little angry, Peter rose and bowed formally to her. "As you wish, of course, Glenna. I am disappointed, and my mother will be, but I only wish for you to be happy." He could not resist murmuring, "I hope you know what you are doing."

"I hope so, too, dear Peter," she whispered as he strode from the room. No doubt it was burning one's bridges which made her feel achingly lonely, with a lump in her throat and her eyes stinging with unshed tears. Ah, well, she would feel better when she had checked on the kitchen.

When she sought out Phoebe, she found her friend curled before the fire in her bedroom. "That looks cozy. May I join you?"

"Do." Phoebe studied Glenna's face and noted the lines of strain. "I heard Peter ordering his carriage for tomorrow. Have you refused him?"

"Yes. I simply could not do it, Phoebe, even though I like him. Was I wrong?"

"I don't suppose so. Certainly it would have been easier for you to accept, so I imagine you had no choice but to follow your inclination." Phoebe gave her friend a quick hug. "I'm glad you will be coming home with me."

"I should not stay long at the vicarage, Phoebe," she protested. "Where would you put my harp?"

"Very amusing," Phoebe retorted. "This time you will have to keep it in your own room. Now your furniture, that's another matter."

Glenna considered the problem. "Mr. Glover might find a place to store it here until I send for it. The harp, too. We can't very well travel with it in a post chaise."

"I'm sure Pontley wouldn't mind if we took his antiquated carriage. Most unsightly, but roomy enough for the harp."

"Yes, let's impose on him," Glenna suggested mischievously, "and take John as our coachman, too."

"And we really should have Mr. Glover for our escort. No, I have it. He can drive a cart with your furniture."

"We shall take Mrs. Morgan for our companion and Mr. Morgan can act as outrider."

"A magnificent procession," Phoebe sighed.

"Still," Glenna said thoughtfully, "I cannot think Pontley would mind if we used the carriage, and sent for the furniture later."

"Peter would say he owes it to you."

"Yes, and Peter would be right. Do you know I have managed to cover almost the whole of the kitchen expenses from my projects?"

"You really were cut out to be someone's housekeeper, Glenna. Now don't take umbrage. I only mean that you have a flair for organization."

"Hmm. Perhaps you are right. Well, I shall write to Pontley to congratulate him on his engagement, and ask if we may use the carriage."

TWELVE

Manner Hall
30 November 1804

My dear Lord Pontley: The work here is nearly completed and I shall be leaving in a short time, I think there is no doubt that you can find a tenant now. Phoebe showed me the announcement of your engagement and we both wish you and Miss Stafford well.

I shall go to the vicarage for a space before returning to Hastings. Would it be acceptable if we used the Manner Hall carriage to transport us there? I will, of course, assume any expense, but we could not fit the harp into a post chaise. Mr. Glover is willing to store my few pieces of furniture until I send for them.

Yours, etc.,
Glenna Forbes

Pontley set the letter down carefully on the center of the blotter. So she was not going to have Westlake after all, it appeared. Probably very unwise of her, considering her situation, but he was relieved. She would not have dealt well with the popinjay, for all his wit and wealth. An idle life would bore her to finders before a month was out. A commotion in the hall interrupted his thoughts and he reluctantly pushed back his chair and rose to meet the latest crisis wrought by Miss Jennifer Stafford.

"Philip, you must train your servants to admit me at any time," she announced as she burst through the library door.

"No, my dear, I am not willing to do that. You might catch me in my bath."

A slight flush crept up her creamy skin, and she adopted a haughty air to cover her embarrassment. "I would hardly invade your bedroom, and I cannot like it when you speak so."

"Very well, I shall make a point of never mentioning my bath again." His solemn tone was belied by the laughter in his eyes, but Jennifer was not amused.

"My aunt is very angry with me," she confessed, taking hold of one of his hands. "Pray tell her that I may dress as I please. Nothing could be more vexatious than having her pinch at me all the time. She is much worse than my parents or my sister."

"Aunt Gertrude has very strong feelings about how a young lady should behave, Jennifer, and wearing breeches does not meet them at all. You must abide by her wishes." He ruefully surveyed the schoolboy figure clad in a scarlet page's outfit.

"When I come to live with you—"

"When we are married I will expect you to behave properly, my dear. Oh, I will not make you burn your favorite costume, but you cannot wear it indiscriminately, either. We are expecting a visitor this morning and your chosen raiment is not acceptable. Please go and change."

There was a flash of rage in the blue eyes turned up to him. He deftly caught the hand pulled back to slap him and held her still for a full minute while he spoke gently to her. "I have no wish to disappoint you, Jennifer. There will probably be time later for us to ride together and you may be a page then if you wish, but now I want you to wear something appropriate. Perhaps the jonquil gown that makes you look like a spring flower," he offered placatingly, as he released her.

Aware that she would not be provided with the opportunity of striking him, she hastily looked about her for some other means of venting her anger and annoying him. Glenna's letter was most immediately to hand and she grabbed it and tore it to shreds while he watched stony-faced. "There," she declared triumphantly. "How does it feel to be paid back for your unkindness?"

"Go and change, Jennifer. If you do not present yourself to Miss Dowell in such a way as to meet with her idea of what is fitting, I will not come to visit you this evening."

Jennifer had long since realized that there was no fate worse than being left alone in her aunt's company for the whole of a long, dreary evening. It was Pontley's habit to dine with them or ride over after dinner to play cribbage or jackstraws with his betrothed. Occasionally he read to them, if Jennifer was not too impatient. "You are punishing me like a child! What do I care if you call or not?" She stamped her foot and glared at him. "I do not have to sit and hear my aunt prattle of my duty. She does not have a very high regard for you, by the way, Philip."

"I am aware of it, my dear, and I assure you it does not bother me in the least. Mrs. Ruffing went through the old schoolroom yesterday and found several items which will interest you—a peepshow with rotating pictures and some puzzles. I had intended to bring them with me this evening."

Jennifer gave in with ill grace. "Oh, very well, but I think you are the greatest bully alive." She swung about on the heels of her riding boots and stalked out of the room, taking care to slam the door after her. Pontley exasperatedly picked up the scattered pieces of his letter and tossed them in the grate. Every encounter with the child-woman had the potential to turn into such a scene, and his patience was wearing very thin. The only thing which cheered him in the entire situation was the knowledge that his aunt's nerves were already entirely frayed. She had long since regretted her interference; since she had come to realize that there was not the least chance of her imposing her own will on her niece, she had taken to unending lectures on behavior which ended, as one might expect, with Jennifer storming from the room and Aunt Gertrude calling for her companion.

Pontley had watched the realization dawning in Lady Pontley that Jennifer was indeed an unstable woman. Although she refused to acknowledge this to him, and perpetually taunted him with his inability to control the girl, he knew she could barely wait to have Jennifer removed from her house. There was no escape from the daily tantrums wrought by the old woman's unbending attitudes. Surely no two people were less likely to live in harmony than the dowager and her niece.

Those soft, whimsical moods which had originally captivated Pontley were not so frequent now, as Jennifer found him less the romantic suitor who would help her escape from her family and find freedom, and more the enforcer of a loose propriety for which she had no regard. Jennifer had begun to chafe at being perpetually in the country; she longed to set London by the ear, and she had no doubt that she could do so. Pontley didn't either, and he was loath to take her there, but had agreed to an expedition of a few days' duration when she pleaded with him in her most appealing manner. They were due to leave, with his aunt, in two days.

Seated once more at the desk he drew forth a sheet of paper and wrote:

Lockwood
5 December 1804

My dear Miss Forbes: I thank you for your good wishes
and for the news that the kitchen is near completion. You
know that there is no necessity for you to leave immediately, but I doubt I could convince you to stay on. The
carriage is at your disposal, and I will send my coachman
as soon as we arrive in London so that he should be with
you in a week.

My regards to Miss Thomas. With her permission I
would like to call on you when you arrive at the vicarage,
to express in person my appreciation for all you have done
at Manner and to introduce you to Miss Stafford.

Yours, etc.,
Pontley

P.S. I trust you have recovered from your affliction.

Glenna looked up from the letter with a crooked grin. "He
does not think we can find our own coachman, Phoebe, and is
sending us his."

"How very thoughtful of him. Does he say anything of
Miss Stafford?"

"Only that he will bring her to call when we are at the vicarage, with your permission, of course. How very proper he
has become! I have no doubt it is Miss Stafford's influence."
Glenna slipped the letter into her reticule and gazed fondly
out the window. "I am going to miss Manner, you know.
There is so much to do in the country."

"*Quite* a different viewpoint than Peter's, my love."

"Yes, he was restless in the few weeks he was here. London is his place, and ever will be. Lady Garth is quite exasperated with me that I would not have him, but perhaps the least bit relieved as well. Not that his engagement or lack of it was the thought uppermost in her mind. There is a much-heralded boy actor coming to London, and she is vexed beyond anything to be in the country at such a time."

"Poor woman," Phoebe retorted unsympathetically. "For all she is kind to you, I do not think you would have had much in common with her either, Glenna."

"No, I suppose not. Well, it cannot matter now." Glenna was always hesitant to raise the subject, because Phoebe did not do so on her own, but she felt compelled to do so now. "We have not seen Captain Andrews in some time."

"I received the impression when last he was here that he would be sailing for a while. It is a pity we will not see him before we leave," she said sadly. Then, unaware that the non sequitur would have any meaning, she blurted out, "How could you ever have become engaged to a naval captain, Glenna? Did it not distress you to think how often he would be away?"

"It was precisely what I wanted, Phoebe," Glenna returned gently. "I did not know Pontley at all well and I really did not particularly wish to marry, so having such a husband appeared to have its merits."

Phoebe regarded her incredulously. "What a scatter-brained scheme."

"Yes, he seemed to think so."

"You *told* him?"

"Not until he had resigned his commission. Then I was very annoyed with him for becoming a viscount with properties to supervise, and in all likelihood being under foot every day."

131

"Sometimes I don't understand you, Glenna. Most ladies would be delighted to wake up one morning and find that they were unexpectedly engaged to a viscount. Not you! Oh, no, you break your engagement."

"I didn't actually break the engagement until I had reason to believe that his affections had been claimed by the el— Miss Stafford."

"Well, you can hardly blame him! Who would not go out and search for another wife when his betrothed callously informed him that she did not wish him about the house?"

"Now, Phoebe, I cannot believe I was so very hard on him. Well, perhaps a little, because he was so . . . so stuffy about the change. He did not consult me or even tell me before he resigned his commission."

"Too, too thoughtless of him," Phoebe mocked. "I suppose he imagined that you would be delighted by his elevation, pleased that he would not be forever away on dangerous missions. Poor, deluded man!"

Glenna choked back a gurgle of laughter. "Pray don't pinch at me, love. It is all in the past now, and settled. Actually he told me the blockade was more dull than dangerous. Captain Andrews said one is as safe in a ship as in a carriage."

"Pooh. That was just because you were nervous when first we boarded. I cannot believe he does not encounter hazards every day. It must be so alarming to be at the mercy of the elements."

"Captain Andrews is a very fine sailor, Phoebe. Pontley said so, and we have ourselves witnessed his skill. I should not worry about him if I were you, love," she suggested gently.

"No, of course not," Phoebe responded stoutly. "I think I shall go and start my packing."

THIRTEEN

The Viscounts Pontley owned a rather small townhouse in London, which it had been the habit in recent years to let out during the season, or for that matter, for whatever part of the year they were able. Pontley's cousin William had frequently been in town but preferred lodgings to the house, as they were more convenient. The most recent occupant of the place had decamped in November and the dowager had suggested, with her usual asperity, that Pontley send an army of servants before them to prepare it. In spite of the fact that the place had been scrubbed, rubbed and brushed, the dowager found fault when they arrived.

"Have the coal cellars been filled? The beds aired? The linen mended? There will be vermin; always are in London. You would think we had let the place to nobodies. I can smell cheroot smoke, and I specifically instructed that there was to be no smoking in the house." She continued with a long list of grievances as she followed the housekeeper up to the room which had been prepared for her. "Come along, Jennifer."

"Yes, aunt. I shall be right with you," her niece murmured demurely. But the moment the old woman's back was turned she stuck out her tongue and grimaced. "It is not a very large place, Philip. I had hoped it would be more elegant. Never mind; I shall try my hand at designing liveries for the servants. Nothing is more impressive than an elegantly livened footman or page."

"No, really? I had no idea it was so important." He regarded her quizzically, but she refused to rise to the bait.

"You haven't the least notion how a luxurious household should be run, my dear Philip."

"Too true, and I haven't a great desire to learn if it is to lead me to Dun territory."

"I wish you would not forever fuss about spending money. I hate a pinch-penny."

He frowned momentarily, but answered lightly, "I have no objection to spending what is reasonable, and what I have. You must tell me what is needed, my dear."

"Oh, I shall." She nodded absently to him and belatedly followed her aunt up the staircase.

Jennifer had marked several gowns in the *Ladies' Monthly Museum* and sent them to her sister's dressmaker in London the previous week, with copious instructions on the colors and fabrics she desired, and her measurements. Pontley was not aware of this, but he was soon enlightened. The day after their arrival he drove the ladies to the dressmaker's establishment and, having no desire to enter the premises, wandered about the cobbled streets until they emerged. The dowager's face was enough to warn him there was trouble brewing; the staggering load of bundles the footman deposited in the carriage certainly startled him. No word was exchanged between the two ladies during the drive home, and the dowager's only comment on entering was, "She is your prospective bride, Pontley. I wash my hands of her."

Such an unpropitious statement led him to take Jennifer into the small parlor where they would not be interrupted. "You seem to have distressed my aunt, Jennifer. Would you enlighten me?"

"She's a stuffy prude, Philip. I have done no more than purchase the most becoming gowns, and all she can do is moan about young ladies wearing white or the softest of pastels, and that it is not decent to wear such low-cut gowns, and that I had no right to have Madame send you the bill without asking you first. White looks totally insipid on me, Philip, as does any pastel, with my fair coloring. And although I have not had a season as yet, I am engaged to be married and there can be no objection to my dressing as I please. Pay no heed to her. You will be positively enchanted with the gowns I have bought."

"And *I* am to pay for." He regarded her with woeful amusement. "I have no objection to doing so, Jennifer, but Aunt Gertrude is right that you should have asked me."

"Am I to ask you for everything, Philip? Shall I need your signature to go shopping?"

"We are not yet married. You will have an allowance, and I will expect you to live within it. If that should prove a problem we will make other arrangements."

Her brow grew stormy. "So you intend to keep me on leading strings, do you? With some niggardly allowance which will hardly cover a pair of dancing slippers or an ivory fan? I have watched your nip-cheese ways, Philip, and you can be sure that I have no intention of imitating you. My father will see that you grant me a sufficient allowance."

"No doubt," he said dryly, remembering the procession he had encountered near Taunton. "I have no intention of being ungenerous, Jennifer, but the estates are not yet in order and I have to be realistic. Will you change into one of your new gowns for me? I should like to see you."

Immediately the cloud lifted from her brow, and she danced over to the door. "It won't take me but a moment. Oh, you will be delighted. Madame said there was never anyone who graced her designs so well." And she was gone.

Pontley tapped impatient fingers on the pianoforte and wished he had some idea of the rules which governed ladies' fashions. How was he to know if the dresses were improper? But when she appeared, he knew. The gown was not seductively low, it was indecent. Of some sort of clinging blue fabric, it hugged her form like the folds of the drapery on a statue. Her ordinarily boyish figure had somehow been rearranged so that there were indeed curves, and there was very little of her breasts left unexposed. He was surprised that she could keep even this little covered, so precarious appeared the design, and he stood speechless before her.

"Is it not stunning? I shall wear it to the theatre tonight and promptly be declared an original. Oh, Philip, I have never been so happy. London will be at my feet, just you wait and see, and you will be so proud of me."

Convinced that more likely he would be a laughingstock, nonetheless he refrained from saying so. It was this perpetual strain of trying to find some middle ground between ruining her simple pleasure, and forcing her to act as she ought, which was wearing him down. In all likelihood she would be taken for a ladybird; he had seen more than one similarly dressed. He cleared his throat. "Very becoming, my dear. The blue perfectly matches your eyes." This once he would let her have her treat, and only hoped that he would not regret it. It seemed doubtful to him that her aunt would be willing to accompany them. "You should change back now so that you will not get it soiled before this evening."

Impulsively she lifted his hand and kissed it. "You cannot know how happy you have made me. I was afraid that you might be as stuffy as my aunt," she admitted engagingly, "but you are famous." Before he could reply she had flitted, spritelike, from the room.

With a shrug of despair he went to seek an interview with the dowager. She was as adamant as he had expected. "I will not accompany you with her dressed like some . . . baggage.

Are you so great a fool as to think what she is wearing accept-able? Have you never been to town before, Pontley?"

"Not often, and I am quite as distressed as you are, my dear aunt, but I do not intend to burst her bubble. Since we became engaged I have done little else, and tonight she shall have her glory. Tomorrow . . . well, I shall see about to-morrow."

"I won't come with you."

Pontley fixed her with a hard, determined stare. "You will accompany us, and do so with a good grace, ma'am."

The dowager shifted her eyes from his and mumbled, "No, I am not well."

His voice was low but insistent. "I have tolerated your snipes and slurs for as long as I intend to, aunt. When you were the only thorn in my flesh I was willing enough to put up with your abuse, for it means nothing to me. I have a far larger problem now, which tries me sorely, and she is your niece. If you wish to see a scandal in your family, of course I cannot convince you to come. But I intend to take Jennifer to the theatre tonight with or without you. If you attend, we will sur-vive the talk; if you do not, we won't. The choice is yours."

"There needn't be any talk at all," she said querulously, "if you would but insist that she wear something decent."

"She shall wear her blue gown. Do you come with us?"

"Yes."

Pontley nodded and left her. She was shaken more by the way he had taken command than by the necessity to accom-pany her niece in that despicable gown. Her last shreds of self-delusion were torn from her; Pontley would not now, or ever, allow her to hold any power at Lockwood or in the family. For all that she despised him, she knew he was twice the man either of her sons had been.

The excursion to the theatre was no less cataclysmic than

any of its participants had expected. The Young Roscius performed to an audience all agog with wonder. Not all of their wonder, however, was reserved for him. Not an eyeglass in the place seemed able to refrain from drifting toward the box where Jennifer sat between the viscount and the dowager. The old woman sat stiffly and made no attempt to converse with her companions. At first Jennifer was delighted to be there and flattered by the attention she drew. Pontley sat at his ease and answered those of her steady stream of questions which he was able.

During the intermissions there were few visitors to their box, since the dowager turned a blind eye to any acquaintance who chanced to be in the audience and, as far as he knew, Pontley did not have any. A few young men who could claim some familiarity with the old woman braved her icy stare to enjoy proximity to Jennifer, but they were not encouraged to linger. Soon Jennifer's exhilaration turned to disappointment and she begged to walk in the corridor so that she might mix with the *ton* and perhaps recognize some friend of her sister's. Pontley agreed, and placed her hand on his arm to lead her from the box. There was a groan from the dowager, but she was not heeded.

The crowd which milled about, unconsciously made a passage for Pontley and his fiancée. Jennifer became more and more conscious of the disapproving stares she raised from the women, and the lecherous ones of the men. Her face drained of color except for two bright spots on her cheeks. When she could bear it no longer, she whispered, "Let us return to the box."

"Certainly, my dear. What do you think of the boy actor? Are you as impressed with him as the rest of town?"

But Jennifer was unable to reply, and merely trembled against his arm. His attention was caught by a former schoolmate who stopped to speak with him. Unable to face the man's obvious interest, Jennifer pulled away from Pontley and fled down the corridor. Although he excused himself to follow as quickly as he could, those in the crowd were pressing back to their seats now and it took him a few minutes to catch up with her. When he did so he found her hiding behind a column, her diminutive body shaken by sobs. He put his arms about her comfortingly and murmured reassurance.

She lifted a horrified face to his and tried to speak but was unable.

"Let me get your aunt," he suggested.

"No. No, please," she sobbed. After a moment she struggled once again to tell him what had happened. "A man . . . grabbed me . . . as I was running. And he . . . *touched* me."

"Poor child. Try not to think on it, Jennifer. He was probably drunk."

"I scratched at his face, and there was blood, and people *saw* me."

"You are all right now, my dear. I am here to take care of you. Would you like to go home now?"

"Yes, please," she whispered.

"Very well. Come to the door of the box and we will get your aunt."

The dowager made no comment on being informed that her niece wished to leave, nor did she hesitate. A cursory glance would have informed her that Jennifer was suffering, but the old woman did not make any sign that she was aware of this. The girl leaned against Pontley's shoulder in the carriage, but shed no more tears. In the light of the hall she blinked uncertainly and watched the dowager's rigid back recede up the stairs.

"Come into the parlor for a moment, Jennifer, and I will

give you a sip of brandy to steady your nerves." She followed him obediently and nestled into a corner of the sofa where she attempted to arrange a wisp of handkerchief over her bosom. Pontley made no comment and refrained from allowing his eyes to stray to the pathetic symbol of modesty. Silently she accepted the glass he offered her and took a few tentative sips before rising. "I should like to go to bed now, sir."

"A maid will be waiting up for you, my dear, so do not hesitate to ask for anything you need." He kissed her brow before she turned and left him.

This subdued, chastened Jennifer he had not seen before and it encouraged him (for the span of twelve hours) to believe that there might be some hope for her. It had been a hard lesson and an ugly one, but she had seemed to gain from the experience. He was rudely disillusioned the next morning.

By now he was familiar with the signs of her tantrums. Whenever there was a commotion in the household he had not the least doubt who was causing it. It was a new experience for the London servants, however, and they stood about in whispering groups. Pontley was led by the shrieks to Jennifer's room, where the door stood open and she was ripping the blue gown to shreds. "I hate it! I hate it!"

Pontley strode into the room and grabbed her by the shoulders. "Stop that. You are making a scene again, Jennifer, and I will not have it."

She stared at him with blazing eyes and screamed, "It is all your fault. I hate you! My aunt knew that such a gown should not be worn by someone of my youth and inexperience. And you let me wear it! Stupid, odious man. It is *your* fault that I was mortified and insulted. I hate you!"

"If you do not control yourself this instant, Jennifer, I will pack you off to Lockwood in the carriage within the hour."

"How can you?" she taunted. "You have sent your wretched coachman off to convey your housekeeper about the countryside."

Pontley came close to striking her then. Only with the greatest effort of will was he able to snarl, "There is no shortage of coachmen in London, Jennifer. Control yourself or leave."

Her bosom rose and fell rapidly, and her hands curled and uncurled, but she was not able to unlock her eyes from his implacable, cold ones. After a space she announced frigidly, "Very well, Philip. If you will please remove yourself from my room, I will dress now."

In the breakfast room the dowager eyed his grim face warily. "What now, Pontley?"

"The future mistress of Lockwood was disposing of her blue gown in her own inimitable way, Aunt Gertrude. After a night's reflection she has come to the conclusion that it was a gross error in my judgment to allow her to wear it. You may be pleased to hear that she praised your good sense in the matter."

"I told you not to let her wear it." There was a tentative note of triumph in the comment.

"So you did. But then, for all the trouble, I find the results more satisfactory this way. I doubt she will have any desire to wear such a gown again. You might even trade on her current charity with you to see that her new purchases are suitably altered. I would bow to your judgment in this case."

"No amount of altering will change their colors," the old woman snapped.

"Then return them."

"You can't do that with a specially made dress, Pontley. They will have to be given away."

"An expensive lesson. The first of many, if I am not mistaken."

They were joined by a sullen Jennifer, who did no more than mumble in reply to any remark addressed to her. Pontley soon excused himself.

For the next two days Jennifer was reasonably well behaved. The dowager, suspicious but grateful, reluctantly agreed to introduce her to some of her friends. Their morning visits were uncommonly successful for Jennifer set out to charm her hostesses, and few could be as charming as Jennifer when she wished to be. Word of her costume at the theatre had gotten about, but the young lady who now appeared in various drawing rooms was discreetly dressed and demure, with an irresistible helplessness which led her to seek one's worldly advice. The Dowager Lady Pontley knew well enough not to be taken in by the confiding, spriteful air, but no one else did. They were issued several invitations for fashionable routs and card parties.

Even at these functions Jennifer disported herself becomingly under her aunt's watchful eye and her affianced husband's solicitous guidance. Pontley was not accustomed to London society and he made no pretense of being familiar with its niceties. There were examples enough to follow, to say nothing of the dowager's pungent comments. He made himself agreeable where it was necessary and formed a friendship or two where he was inclined. One of these men offered to put him up for Watier's, but Pontley was not as yet inclined to delve into London's exclusive clubs. He had quite enough on his hands with Jennifer.

"Well, ride with me in the morning," Mr. Archer suggested. "Nothing clears the head after one of these affairs better than an early morning ride."

Pontley had agreed and found himself the following day in Hyde Park mounted on one of the two hacks he had purchased at Tattersall's. The other, a distinctively marked black mare, he had acquired for Jennifer as a token of his appreciation for her becoming behavior the past few days. She had proved suitably grateful, with a dimpled smile and an impulsive hug.

After the days bound in by the city, Pontley thoroughly enjoyed the ride, a long one which would make him later than usual for breakfast, but since he was always the first in the household to have his meal, it made no difference. Archer proved an interesting companion, conversant on politics and the arts, society and the theatre. As they approached the gates, their attention was claimed by a gathering of people about a young man who appeared to be delivering a speech. Archer called to an acquaintance to ask who it was.

"The boy actor, you know the one. Betty his name is, William Betty. He's doing a scene from Hamlet for his audience," the gentleman replied.

Archer turned to Pontley and asked if he had as yet seen the Young Roscius, but Pontley was not attending to him. He could not take his eyes from the black horse whose reins the boy held; there was no mistaking the distinct white markings on the black mare. With an effort he withdrew his gaze and Archer was struck by the grimness of his expression. "Not impressed with the prodigy, eh, Pontley? Haven't seen him yet myself, but there's no going anywhere in town where they aren't talking of him. Shall we ride over?"

"No. That is, you may if you wish but I have no desire to see him."

"I have tickets for the theatre this evening and I'm devilish sharp-set, so I'll give it a pass."

The two men rode on and Pontley was grateful when their

ways diverged a short distance from the entrance. He retraced his route into the park and rode close enough to the gathering to have an excellent view of the young man. It was indeed Jennifer, tricked out in a young man's dress and cleverly made up to bear an incredible likeness to the actor. Her voice, too, carried a good distance (probably from years of practice screaming, he thought mournfully) and she was reciting Hamlet's speeches as though she were born to the role. It was a matter of astonishment to him, though, that she was able to fool the gathering, since many of its number must have seen the boy perform. She was nearing the completion of a monologue and he placed himself where she could not fail to see him. When her eyes met his there was a glint of defiance in them, and he was not sure that she would obey the beckoning gesture he made.

Jennifer had begun to wonder how to extract herself from her prank, for it seemed likely that this partisan crowd would follow her when she attempted to leave the park. More from self-preservation than from a desire to obey her fiancé, she made an elaborate bow to the hearty applause, sprang onto her mare like a boy and joined Pontley. Together they rode from the park without a word, and quickly lost themselves in the maze of streets beyond. It was not until they neared the house in Brook Street that he spoke.

"You appeared to be enjoying yourself, Jennifer."

Her chin lifted stubbornly. "I was, and it did no one any harm."

"I dare say. And yet you rode out alone, which was not only improper but might have been dangerous."

"You bought the horse for me to amuse myself, Philip."

Another expensive lesson, he thought. "I am not sure the Young Roscius would appreciate being imitated, and your performance, though excellent, did not perhaps reach his standards. What if someone had attempted to expose you as a fraud?"

She gave a nervous giggle. "I had them all fooled, as you could see. Much leeway is given for the lack of costume and scenery, my dear fellow. And I thought my disguise admirable."

"You look enough like him to pass as a double. Where did you come by the clothes?"

"Oh, that was a simple matter. I asked a footman to purchase me an outfit, as I wished to surprise my brother with it. When I told him my brother was younger but about the same size, he came up with these and they fit very well."

"And I suppose the bill will be sent to me."

"Of course. Well, I have no money of my own left, Philip," she confided, "and they were not so very expensive. No so much as one of my gowns."

Pontley assisted her to dismount before the waiting groom, who nervously cast a worried look at his lordship. The groom had attempted to refuse Miss Stafford when she arrived at the stables in a boy's costume demanding that her new horse be saddled, and not with a sidesaddle, either. She had railed at him like a fishwife, and since Lord Pontley was out and could not be consulted, he had done as she bid. The viscount did not now reprimand him but led the young lady back to the house, where they were directed to the dowager, who smoldered in the breakfast room. She had long since been informed that Jennifer was not in the house, and had not left with the viscount. As she studied the girl's costume, her face became more sour than usual, her eyes filled with fury.

"You have been abroad in that outfit, Jennifer? And you permitted it, Pontley?"

"I had nothing to say to it, Aunt. Jennifer conceived the

idea of passing herself off as the actor Betty in the park, where I found her."

The young lady's face became mulish. "There was no harm in it, Aunt Gertrude. No one suspected that I was not the real actor."

"Have you no shame? Parading about as a boy, calling notice to yourself in the park? You are intent on disgracing your family and yourself! What if word of this gets about? Not a drawing room in town will be open to you! We scarcely live down one incipient scandal when you must throw yourself into another. And don't look to me to save you from disgrace, missy. One day your cozening smile will no longer work for you with anyone, you will be so far beyond the pale." She turned in her fury on Pontley. "You must control the chit. Have her locked in her room, if it is necessary, but do not let her go about town casting shame on us all."

"I would remind you, dear aunt, that I am not yet married to Miss Stafford. She is presently under your chaperonage."

"Then as her chaperone I insist that we retire to the country immediately. The next time she comes to London it will have to be under your aegis, Pontley, where her behavior cannot reflect on me."

Jennifer wailed her anger at such a decision, but Pontley bowed and agreed. "I can be ready to leave whenever you wish, ma'am, but I would remind you that as your niece, Miss Stafford's behavior is like to reflect on you always."

The old woman gave a shudder of repulsion. "I will be ready to leave in two hours."

It was vexing beyond anything for Jennifer to be discussed as though she were not present. She grasped a cup and flung it at Pontley's head, which it grazed slightly. His lips compressed into a hard line. "Get to your room and see that your maid begins packing immediately, Jennifer. I will not hesitate to have you carried to the carriage if you are not ready or willing."

Jennifer knew she had gone too far, but she did not apologize. Instead she glared at him and stomped from the room. Pontley immediately summoned a footman and gave instructions for a departure. When they were alone again he turned to the dowager. "I would suggest, ma'am, that you have a close watch kept on your niece until we depart, since I do not think it beyond her in her present frame of mind to try to run away. It would matter nothing to her that she has nowhere to go."

Even Lady Pontley was shocked by this suggestion, but she realized that it was not an impossibility, and she accorded him a bitter nod before stiffly leaving the room. Pontley, as usual, was forced to keep at bay the thought that this sort of crisis was now a permanent feature of his life. It would become no better on their marriage, and perhaps worse.

FOURTEEN

Mrs. Morgan blew her nose repeatedly, and Betsey's eyes were wet with tears when Glenna bid them farewell. She took a last look about the house as nostalgically as though she had lived there the better part of her life rather than a few months. Mr. Glover saw that there was a ham for the vicarage loaded into the carriage, and assured Glenna that her furniture would be well cared for. The sun broke through an overcast day as the two young ladies climbed into the carriage and they waved forlornly to the group who had made their stay so pleasant. No longer was the carriage-way overgrown with grass, nor the brambles so wild as to scratch the sides of a vehicle passing along it. The grounds were manicured and the hedges trimmed, and just before they were out of sight of the far coppice they had a glimpse of a deer.

"Do you suppose it was ours?" Phoebe asked sadly.

"I'm sure of it, love," Glenna responded with a bracing smile. "Come now, you must look forward to being home again, to seeing your mama and papa."

"Yes, of course. It is just that . . . Burgess Hill is so far from here."

Although Glenna understood her to be saying that Burgess Hill was so far from Captain Andrews, she made no effort to allude to that subject. "You have been an angel to stay with me so long. We have had a pleasant time, haven't we? I've grown accustomed to being mistress of an establishment, Phoebe, and do not look forward to finding lodgings."

"Have you no relations you wish to visit? It pains me to

think of you in some shabby rooms in Hastings, in spite of all your friends there. Why don't you go to the Stokeses for a while? I know they would be happy to have you."

"It would only delay my establishing myself somewhere. Do you suppose at my age I need have a companion?"

Phoebe regarded her incredulously. "Well, of course you do. Surely you had not thought to live alone."

"I would prefer it, but I believe you are right. What a nuisance! Have you ever met a companion who was not bird-witted, Phoebe?"

"Never."

"Nor have I. There is no use in dwelling on it now, however. Shall I read for a while?"

Thus their journey progressed as pleasantly as possible, and if Glenna occasionally allowed her mind to stray to how she was to go on in the future, it was not to be wondered at. Phoebe had spells of melancholy as well, but they worked to keep one another's spirits up, and arrived at the vicarage to a warm welcome. Pontley's coachman was thanked and an unsuccessful attempt made to reward him for his services. His instructions were to deliver the carriage to Lockwood and then take the stage coach to London, so the young ladies saw that their belongings were quickly removed to the house.

There was a surprise awaiting them at the vicarage in the person of a young man they had both known years ago when he had lived there with the vicar as his tutor. Although it was seven years since Phoebe had seen him, she would have recognized the boyish face anywhere. "Carlton! Whatever are you doing here?"

The vicar interrupted to say, "It is Lord Kilbane now, my dear, and we are honored to have his lordship spend the holiday with us. There is not time for him to get to Ireland this year for his break."

"Well, I am delighted to see you again. Isn't this famous, Glenna? Now we can put on a theatrical." Phoebe extended her hand to the young man, who was almost a brother to her.

Lord Kilbane grinned and murmured, "Always a pleasure to see you, Miss Thomas. I remember our theatricals as among the most cherished hours of my stay here." He turned apologetically to the vicar. "Not that I did not relish my lessons, of course, sir."

Since Kilbane had not and never would be a scholar, his statement was viewed with amusement, but he was an engaging young man whose kind heart, easy-going manner and ready laugh made his passage through the vicarage a matter of pleasure for all its occupants. When he turned to Glenna, there was a sparkle in his eyes. "And Miss Forbes. I had not thought to be reunited with you when I wrote to invite myself to the vicarage." He turned suddenly serious. "I understand you lost your father last summer. Please accept my condolences; I realize how close you were."

"Thank you, Lord Kilbane. I know you understand what such a loss is." It was more than three years since the young man's father had died, but he nodded agreement and pressed her hand. Glenna, like Phoebe, had always considered him in the light of a younger brother. At twenty-one he was grown more handsome and the black curly hair was kept more neatly, but the boyish enthusiasm of the fourteen-year-old had not diminished. He spoke irreverently of his life at Cambridge as they entered the house, and even the vicar could not resist a chuckle.

Phoebe willingly agreed to share her room with Glenna, as there was only the one spare bedroom at the vicarage, but she muttered as they entered, "Not your harp, please. It will have to take its place in the drawing room as before."

"I cannot think the vicar will mind, since I intend to be

here for a few weeks this time. I remarked no astonishment when it was carried into the house."

"They are becoming used to your idiosyncrasies, my dear," Phoebe retorted.

"Such tolerance. I shall have to acquit myself well to repay it."

"Do you know, I think that is the perfect solution." Phoebe stared off into space for a moment before enlightening her friend. "Papa has been fretting about funds for the village school, and I think we could help him. Remember we did so once years ago? Oh, it needn't be a great production, just a short program with you playing the harp and a drama of no great length. Lord Kilbane would surely enter into our scheme, and we could each play several parts if it were a farce."

"But Kilbane and I won't be here very long, Phoebe."

"We could have it just after Christmas, when everyone is still in the country. If we choose something *worthy*, it is bound to be of great length, so we will have a light sort of play. More folks would be interested in that in any case."

"Even a light play, as you call it, would be too long for the three of us to handle in such a short time, I fear."

"No, listen, I have it. Did your cousin Mary Stokes ever send you the charming satire she did on country house parties?"

"Yes," Glenna grinned. "I had no idea she had so sharp a tongue, or that she would exert herself to scribble it down not once but any number of times to send to her friends."

"Well, she didn't, you know. I have it on the best authority that she paid the governess at Wattings five shillings a copy to do so for her. Never mind that. Don't you think it would be perfect? Kilbane could act Squire Irascible and Mr. Hedgehead. He would adore those parts."

"Show me your copy, love. I do not remember it so well as you do." Glenna had caught Phoebe's enthusiasm, and the two were soon poring over the very delightful sketch. It had the advantage of containing only three short acts (Mary Stokes would hardly have written more), with only half a dozen players, and was just the sort of production to appeal to the neighbors around Burgess Hill. Phoebe soon rose, declared her intention of confirming the project with her parents, and departed.

By the following day the participants had begun rehearsals in the drawing room, which was graciously relinquished for their endeavors. There were several places in the script where they were obliged to make changes because they had not enough actors—an irksome chore, but necessary. While they were puzzling over this, a note was delivered from Pontley asking if he and Miss Stafford might call that afternoon.

Phoebe's brows drew together with concern. "Oh, Lord, Glenna, he has already returned from London, and we had his coachman. How inconvenient for him, but he does not even mention the circumstance."

"Who is he?" Kilbane asked, his curiosity piqued that the ladies had been driven to the vicarage by someone's coachman.

"*You* explain to him, Glenna. I would make it sound ridiculous," Phoebe asserted.

"It is a very simple matter, Lord Kilbane—"

"Spare me the 'Lord,' if you please, both of you."

"Yes, well, last winter I became engaged to a Captain Philip Hobart of the Royal Navy. In the spring his cousin, Viscount Pontley, died, and about the same time they learned that the younger cousin had died in India in the autumn. So he became the eighth Viscount Pontley. I broke the engagement a while after that and of course had nothing further to

152

do with him. But when my father died last summer Pontley came and suggested that I live at his estate in Somerset and oversee the renovations he wished undertaken there. Phoebe went with me and when we were ready to leave he sent his coachman to drive us back." She turned to Phoebe to murmur, "I see nothing ridiculous in it."

"It depends on how much of it you tell, of course," Phoebe agreed with laughing eyes, before turning to Kilbane. "Lord Pontley lives at Lockwood, perhaps ten miles from here. I shall certainly agree to their call, Glenna, so that we may thank him for the coachman."

While she penned a cordial note to Pontley, the Irishman asked Glenna about Miss Stafford. "She is his fiancée, and niece of his uncle's wife. We have not met her, either, but I understand she is a charming young lady. No doubt she is staying with the dowager until the wedding." Glenna was tempted to tell him her opinion of the dowager, but decided against it.

They had just determined the division of parts some hours later when the viscount was announced and entered the drawing room with a remarkably attractive girl in a demure blue driving costume. The vicar and Mrs. Thomas welcomed them and introduced Lord Kilbane. Miss Stafford acknowledged the introductions to each member with a shy, trusting smile, her eyes alight with interest. When Mrs. Thomas drew the girl into conversation, Pontley took the opportunity to speak with Glenna and Phoebe.

"I understand your journey was uneventful and you both appear to be in the best of health." His eyes dwelled for a moment on Glenna's restored looks, and there was an unmistakable glint in them.

Phoebe hastened to express their gratitude for his coachman and the Manner Hall coach. "We could not have managed Glenna's harp without it, of course, but we had no idea of infringing on your use of your own coachman. I felt alarmed to hear that you had returned from London already, for you must have needed him."

"We managed very well without. Our departure from town was earlier than we expected."

"I do hope through no indisposition of the Dowager Lady Pontley," Glenna offered sweetly, convinced that this should repay him for his mockery.

His serious expression startled her. "No, not an indisposition. She is quite well, thank you, and I will tell her that you inquired."

"Does Miss Stafford stay with her at the dower house?" Phoebe asked curiously. "And has a date been set for the wedding?"

"Miss Stafford stays with her aunt, yes, and the date of the wedding depends on when Sir George and Lady Stafford can join us here. It is hunting season, you know," he remarked dryly.

"You are to be married at Lockwood?" Phoebe was surprised and did not attempt to conceal it.

"All agreed it would be simplest as there is to be only the family."

Jennifer approached him impetuously and cried, "Oh, Philip, the most wonderful thing! They are going to do a play written by Miss Forbes's cousin and have just been choosing parts. Lord Kilbane assures me there would be a part for me if I should like it." She threw the young Irishman a look of sheer ecstasy and a smile which made her dimples peek out. "It would be necessary for them to change the script if they did not have another lady, and that would be such a shame! Do say I may join them, do!"

"Jennifer, you have not considered that they must rehearse daily and you are situated some miles from here." His voice was gentle, persuasive, but his eyes were wary. Nothing would be worse than for her to have a tantrum here.

"Oh, pooh! I could ride over every day on that adorable mare you got for me. She will need the exercise and I should love it." A flash of annoyance lit her eyes briefly at his unrelenting expression, but she controlled it to say, "If you did not wish to accompany me, of course I would bring a groom. No harm would come of it."

Pontley was torn with indecision. It was galling to be forever denying her those treats she most wished, but he could envision her losing her temper under the strain of repeated rehearsals. Her histrionic abilities he did not doubt after her imitation of Roscius, but her ability to apply herself for a lengthy period of time to any project was more suspect.

Unexpectedly, support for the plan came from Glenna. "Do let her join us, Lord Pontley. We have chosen an amusing play, very short, written by my cousin Mary Stokes, and we have no intention of being in the works for more than two weeks. Both Lord Kilbane and I will be leaving early in the new year."

When Pontley reluctantly assented, Jennifer squeezed his arm in a child's gesture of approbation. "You are the dearest man, and I promise you I shall be on my very best behavior."

"Your aunt will have to agree as well, Jennifer."

"I'm sure she will be delighted to have me out of the house," she retorted with a saucy smile.

Kilbane approached with their only copy of the play and suggested that they decide which role she would fill. "Perhaps you would like to read it first. We have been doubling up on characters, so I doubt it makes any difference to any of us which character you choose. Lord Pontley might be interested in joining us as well."

"Thank you, no. I fear I have not the least talent for acting." Pontley was looking for a way to extract Glenna from the group so that he might speak with her. When a visitor was announced for the vicar, the young people decided to appropriate the dining parlor for the time being so that they could familiarize Miss Stafford with the play and help her choose a part. "Might I have a word with you, Miss Forbes, before you join the others?"

"You will want to know how we left Manner Hall," she suggested and urged the others to go along without her, which they were more than willing to do. "We might walk in the garden; there really is nowhere else." She made a helpless gesture to indicate the size of the vicarage and went to fetch her pelisse.

There was a threat of snow in the air, but the ground was dry and the air crisp. Glenna led Pontley through the shrubbery to the garden paths beyond, where there was little enough to be seen but the empty beds and forlorn bare trees. "I wish you had let us pay your coachman, sir. He would not take a thing."

"Those were his instructions, Miss Forbes, and you may rest easy that he has been rewarded for his diligence in seeing you and Miss Thomas safely here."

"We thank you for your kindness, but certainly it was enough to lend us the carriage for such a long trip. Now it will have to be returned to the Hall."

"I'm not worried about that, so you needn't trouble yourself."

Glenna could only nod under his direct gaze. "The kitchen is delightful, you know. Betsey cannot sufficiently sing its praises and produced the most delectable dishes to show her appreciation. The painting was completed some weeks ago, and we left with the grounds vastly improved, if not perfect. Mr. Glover insisted on sending a ham to the vicarage. I hope you don't mind."

"I'm pleased that he thought of it. The vicar and his wife have been kind in sparing their daughter to you for so long."

"Phoebe disliked leaving as much as I did," Glenna said incautiously.

Pontley stopped walking and turned to face her. "I told you to stay on, Miss Forbes. There was no need to leave so soon."

"No, no, I didn't mean we felt forced to leave. Phoebe's parents wanted her home for Christmas and there was no reason for me to stay there. All I meant to say was that we both enjoyed being there and appreciate your offering us the opportunity."

He waved aside her thanks and resumed their walk, his hands dug into his pockets. "What will you do now?"

"After I leave the vicarage? I still have not decided precisely. Originally I thought to take lodgings in Hastings, but that would mean having a companion, you know, and the thought does not appeal to me."

"You would have been better off if you had married Westlake."

"Undoubtedly, but I did not wish to do so," she replied coldly.

"Thought he'd be too much underfoot, I dare say. But I cannot think he would have interfered with your independence, Miss Forbes. He didn't strike me as a very *forceful* man."

This time it was Glenna who paused. "I am not interested in your opinion of Mr. Westlake, Pontley. Shall we return to the house?"

"I meant no offense, Miss Forbes. Come, walk a little further with me. Miss Stafford will not be ready to leave yet and I would merely cast a damper on her enjoyment if I joined the group."

Glenna shrugged off her irritation. "I imagine life is a little dull for her at Lockwood, especially with your aunt. You don't mind her joining our theatricals, do you?"

"Not much. As you say, she is in need of a diversion."

"Her enthusiasm is infectious. She's like a—"

"An elf, I believe you called her once, Miss Forbes."

A flush rose to her cheeks. "I was quoting you, my lord. For myself I should have used 'pixie.' "

"She is certainly in tearing spirits right now, but she does come down from alt eventually. Her . . . nerves are . . . delicate, and, aside from the daily ride over here, I most fear the strain that a performance would put on her. You must let me know if the burden appears too great for her."

His consideration for his fiancée inexplicably moved Glenna and the lump in her throat made it impossible for her to do more than nod. She bent down to pick off the withered head of a dead flower but could not decide what to do with it, and stood staring at it for a moment. Pontley took it from her hand and tossed it into the field beyond. "Your cheeks are rosy from the cold," he said gently. "Shall we head back?"

Afraid that she would appear uncivil if she did not soon offer some conversation, she cast wildly about her mind for a subject. "I brought the mare with me and have stabled her in the village, since they have no stable here. If I take lodgings in Hastings . . . Well, that is one of the reasons I would rather not. To part with her would be awful, but if I must, then I will give her back to you."

"I would be happy to keep her for you at any time, but perhaps you should think of visiting in the country. Your cousin who wrote this play, could you not stay with her?"

"Mary Stokes? I don't know. Her family is in Hampshire,

near Alton, and I suppose they would not mind my coming, but it would be no permanent solution. I will not plunk myself down on my relations and be one of those guests you cannot dispose of. Before I stayed at Manner Hall I was perfectly content to return to Hastings and pick up my life there. Now it seems such a *useless* thing to do." She smiled tentatively at him and tossed up a disparaging hand. "You see, I am become even more opinionated and perverse. I enjoyed having something to do, and I would not even have Papa's papers to work on now in Hastings, as I donated them to the University at his request. I beg your pardon! How stupid of me to belabor you with my concerns. I never meant to."

"I am honored that you are so frank with me and I only wish I had an answer to your problems." His brow was troubled and he slowed his pace while he considered her dilemma.

"Oh, please, think no more of my crotchets," she begged, embarrassment overcoming her. "You have been kindness itself, and Phoebe assures me that I was very callous in my treatment of you. I am pleased that all has worked out so well on your behalf."

It seemed impossible to Pontley that Miss Forbes, for all her sense and discernment, should not have immediately divined Miss Stafford's true character. Though he had been duped for several weeks on his first visit to Huntley, he had somehow believed that Miss Forbes would take in at a glance what he had failed to see for so long. Had she not determined that Peter Westlake, although a nice enough young man, would not suit her as a husband? And that decision made even in the light of the problems she now faced? He wished to shake her, and hold her, but he merely said, "Indeed."

"Do you know," she continued, unaware of his troubled thoughts because she did not dare look at him, "I think I will write to Mary. She will be so pleased that we are to perform her play and might even make the effort to attend our performance. If she were to come here I might return with her to Hampshire for a spell, but I will *not* begin a tour of my relations. Other than Mary and her family there are no close ones, in any case." She offered him a forced smile of assurance. "Phoebe suggested I should visit the Stokeses, too."

"And could you take the horse there?"

"Oh, yes, it would be an ideal place to have her. Mary hardly ever rides but her father and brother do, so I should have company." They were approaching the house now and could see the young people through the dining parlor window. Phoebe and Kilbane were laughing at something Miss Stafford had done or said, and it looked a very merry gathering. Glenna turned impulsively to Pontley and lay a hand on his arm. "You need not worry about the play, you know. There is nothing improper about it—just tongue in cheek abuse of country house parties."

He laid his hand briefly over hers before she removed it. "I was not in the least worried, Miss Forbes, and I far prefer that it be a comedy to a heavy drama."

They entered through the long windows which Phoebe obligingly opened for them, and Miss Stafford triumphantly announced to Pontley that she was to be Miss Glimmer. "You will like the play, Philip, as it is truly diverting. There are all these women discussing each other's characters when one is absent, but mostly they deplore the niggardly meals and the fact that the men are forever out hunting. There is a great deal of discussion about a Mr. Brunt, who never even appears! And when the ladies aren't raking one another over the coals they are writing letters, all day long, to everyone and anyone who isn't there, vowing they are missing the most delightful event." She turned shyly to Glenna and asked, "You

160

will not mind that I am to be Miss Glimmer?"

"Most assuredly not!" Glenna protested with a laugh. "Phoebe surely told you I was sadly put out to be cast as a youngster at my advanced years. Mrs. Snip will do very well for me."

Kilbane gave a hoot of laughter, but Phoebe hushed him. "You may have one of my parts, if you like. I am left with Cornelia Chaos and Lady Lump and would be just as pleased to have only one."

"No, if you wish for me to play the harp, I think one role will be more than enough. Phoebe, shall we invite Mary Stokes to attend our performance? I could stay with Mrs. Carter for a night or two."

"Yes, do. Would you go back with her?"

"I have a mind to, for a while." She glanced at the scattered sheets on the mahogany dining table. "We should make another copy of the play so that Miss Stafford may take it home with her next time she comes."

"Please, you are all to call me Jennifer," the girl said happily, "and tomorrow, if I may come then, I will copy down my own speeches."

Phoebe said she would be welcome any time, and was roundly seconded by Kilbane. In an effort to prove her sincerity in her promise of good behavior, Jennifer allowed Pontley to draw her away then without the least demur.

FIFTEEN

Glenna found the next few days fully occupied with the play and her endeavors to crochet a shawl for Phoebe for Christmas without being surprised in her task. Jennifer Stafford came daily, with a groom, and seldom wavered in her delight in the project. It was in her role as Miss Glimmer that she was expected to flirt with Kilbane in his role as Mr. Hedgehead. There was a good deal of amusement over this interaction at first, but Glenna became aware of a subtle difference in Kilbane's attitude before long. When originally he had appeared enchanted with Jennifer, she had been not the least alarmed, as it seemed to her natural that anyone would be with such a sprite. But Glenna became uncomfortable when she witnessed his deepening attachment and constant attentions to the girl.

"I think we have put the cat among the pigeons," she announced one night as she brushed her hair for bed. "Kilbane is completely star-struck with the girl and I hate to see him hurt. I think Jennifer is too young to realize that she is encouraging him, and besides, it is flattering to have such admiration as his."

"Nonsense," Phoebe replied with asperity. "She knows precisely what she is doing and does not care a fig if he is hurt."

Glenna was startled by her vehemence, and turned to confront her friend. "Whatever are you saying, Phoebe? Have you taken the girl in dislike?"

"Oh, it's impossible not to like her, with her gaiety and eagerness. She reminds me of a particularly adorable puppy. But I will not believe that she is so naive as to be unaware of what she is doing. Kilbane is like a brother to me, Glenna, and I could kick him for being so blind. The girl is engaged to Lord Pontley, very soon to be wed, and what does Kilbane do but lose his heart to her. I came in this afternoon to hear her confiding to him in the most pathetic way that her aunt does not treat her with any affection. He looked as though he would gallop off to confront the old lady with his ferocious anger. To me it is not laughable," she finished mournfully.

"I cannot imagine the old dragon treating anyone with affection, but surely Pontley makes up for that." Glenna did not meet Phoebe's eyes in the glass.

Phoebe studied her friend critically. "What makes you think he would know how to handle such a spirited child? I have never heard you acclaim him for his tenderness. Jennifer confided to *me* that he is very strict with her, never allowing her to ride alone, even on the estate. And when he is displeased with her he does not come to dine and spend the evening with her and her aunt. You can be sure she has told her tale to Kilbane, too, for his sympathy. I tell you, Glenna, so long as she has someone to fuss over her and shower her with praise, she has not the least concern for whom she hurts."

For some time Glenna had fought to conceal this knowledge from herself, but now she was forced to acknowledge it. She had watched Jennifer as closely as Phoebe had, and her heart ached for Pontley when she realized that the girl was selfish to a degree. No word of praise for Pontley escaped the girl's lips unless he had done something to especially please her, and then she spoke of it off-handedly, as though it were her due. Although it was not difficult for Glenna to see how Pontley had fallen in love with the child (did she not have Kilbane's example daily before her eyes?), she foresaw an uneasy future for them. Oh, Jennifer probably returned his love as far as she was able, but Glenna doubted the tenuous nature of such an affection would provide Pontley with the happiness he deserved. Jennifer's affections were freely given to anyone who returned them at the time, and the viscount was sure to be continually wounded by such a weathervane. Glenna uttered a dispirited sigh. "She is but a child, after all. Perhaps she will grow out of her selfishness."

"And what of Kilbane in the meantime, Glenna? Are you willing to sit back and watch him make a fool of himself?"

"I really cannot see what I can do, Phoebe, or you either. We are not likely to be able to break the spell she has cast over him, and he would not thank you for interfering, I am as anxious as you that she not hurt him or Pontley. Remember, Kilbane will return to Cambridge in a few weeks, and Jennifer will soon be married."

"You must speak with Pontley," Phoebe said stubbornly.

Glenna was horrified at the thought and cast her hands up in despair. "What would you have me say to him, my dear? Let me see. How about, 'Pontley, you must treat Miss Stafford with greater affection so that she will not seek solace elsewhere'? No, I have it. How about, 'Pontley, you clumsy ox, you are making as great a botch of your second engagement as you did of your first'?"

A reluctant chuckle escaped Phoebe, but she said sternly, "It is no laughing matter, Glenna."

"I know, but you can hardly expect me to give advice to him, love. Be reasonable. When he sees how impressive Kilbane's attentions are to her, he will be moved to imitate them and she will not need Kilbane's worship."

"And how is he to see them if he never accompanies her?"

"You might have your mother invite him to dine," Glenna suggested impassively.

"Very well, but I hope you realize we would have to include the dowager."

"Oh, Lord, I had not thought of that. Perhaps it would not be a good idea . . ."

"No, but as it is the only thing you can suggest, we will have to make the best of it."

Glenna experienced an unwonted exasperation with her friend. "For the life of me, Phoebe, I cannot see how you blame this whole mess on me and expect me to find the means of remedying it."

"If you had married Pontley this would never have happened," her friend retorted.

"Your reasoning is impeccable, Phoebe. I will bid you good night."

The invitation to dine was sent with Jennifer the next day, and on the following one came Pontley's acceptance on behalf of himself, his fiancée and the dowager. Jennifer did not appear to be overjoyed by the treat, and Phoebe was skeptical, but it was Kilbane and Glenna who were most wary. Kilbane had no desire to be faced with the betrothed and the aunt of his little jewel, and Glenna could have lived her life through without seeing the dowager and had no regrets. Only the vicar and Mrs. Thomas were oblivious to the undercurrents, and they were so blissfully unaware that Phoebe was almost distressed for them.

The party from Lockwood arrived in a sedate landau with a scarlet-and-gold-liveried coachman. Jennifer deplored the former and confessed with great pride that she had just designed the latter's outfit. The Dowager Lady Pontley scowled at her and muttered something about Pontley's indulgence of the girl's whims, but the viscount himself paid no heed to her remark. Assembled in the drawing room, Kilbane set himself to amuse the dowager while Pontley conversed with the vicar and his wife. Jennifer described to Phoebe and Glenna in extravagant detail the plans she had for further liveries in her future household.

"For I see not the least reason, do you, why they should all be dressed alike. What would be most impressive on a tall footman would appear dumpy on a short coachman. And pages. Now, Philip has not a single page in the entire household and I have told him that they are essential. Silver and blue, I think, with large coins for buttons and huge, old-fashioned buckles on their shoes. And I shall have a blue mantelet trimmed with a silvery fur so that when I go out driving and they are standing behind it will make quite a picture." She changed the subject abruptly when she found her aunt's piercing gaze on her. "Do you think we might have a rehearsal after dinner to show Philip and Aunt Gertrude how we progress?"

Phoebe agreed that it would be useful for them to accustom themselves to an audience; Glenna received an imperious beckon from the dowager, which she reluctantly obeyed, displacing Kilbane, who was just as glad to join Jennifer.

"Miss Stokes, I believe," the dowager said coldly.

"You must forgive my little deception, Lady Pontley. I had no other thought than to assist you in your time of trouble." Glenna could not summon up the smile she wished, but she met the old woman's eyes calmly.

"You were a very inadequate companion with your determined ways. I find Miss Perkins much more to my taste."

Glenna wondered if Miss Perkins was bird-witted, but she did not ask. "I hope you find yourself comfortable in the dower house, my lady. It must be a pleasure to have your niece visiting you."

The dowager eyed her suspiciously, looking for a sign of mockery, but there was no trace of it in Glenna's face. "Humph. I am too old to cater to the whims of youth, Miss Forbes, and will be delighted when she moves to the main house."

"I understand they await only Miss Stafford's parents from the north."

"That could be weeks more," the old woman grumbled. "My brother lives and breathes hunting at this time of year and his wife takes forever to get her procession on the road."

"Does Miss Stafford's sister come, too?"

"If she isn't breeding again," the dowager sniffed.

Glenna was at a loss to respond to such a remark, so she turned the conversation. "We have just decided to rehearse the play for you after dinner. Miss Stafford is excellent in her role, and I feel sure you and Lord Pontley will be proud of her."

Since dinner was announced then, the dowager had no chance to make the acrid reply she intended and Glenna was spared further discourse with her. Owing to the uneven numbers of men and women, Jennifer was seated between the dowager and Kilbane, who kept her flattering attention throughout the meal. Pontley made polite conversation with Mrs. Thomas and watched the couple opposite him with an expression Glenna could not decipher. When the ladies withdrew, Phoebe whispered to her friend, "He does not seem to be the least affected by Kilbane's courting of the girl, nor her obvious partiality for him."

"Well, you would hardly expect Pontley to make a scene, Phoebe. I am convinced he has taken note of it."

"And who has not? The dowager is wearing the sourest face ever I saw, and I pity Jennifer when she is alone with her aunt this evening."

"That does not worry me near so much as the troubled frowns your parents are exhibiting. I think they had no idea before now of what is going forward."

"Poor Mama. She will blame herself for allowing such a hobble under her roof, and you can be sure Papa will have a serious, painful discussion with Kilbane in the library. Oh, I could ring Jennifer's neck."

"She is not alone to blame, Phoebe. Kilbane is old enough to know better than to act such a gudgeon." Glenna made a gesture of silence as they joined the other ladies in the drawing room, but soon all three of the younger women left to search Phoebe's room for props for their performance.

Jennifer's aunt took the opportunity to put some rather embarrassing questions to Mrs. Thomas on the nature of their young visitor. Under cover of righteous indignation she solicited Kilbane's background and association with the Thomas family. "An Irish peer," she snorted haughtily. "There is something approaching frivolity in the lot of them. Others may be impressed with their good humor and ease of manner, but just see where it leads," she said significantly. "*I* call it a want of conduct."

Mrs. Thomas, appalled by this attack, could think of little to say, and it was fortunate that the men joined them at that moment. There was no sign that any such disagreeable conversation had taken place over their port for, although the vicar still appeared worried, the other two men showed no evidence of less than pleasantness. When everyone was reassembled and the necessary props gathered, Phoebe introduced the play, and with Mrs. Thomas acting as prompter, they went through it almost without a hitch.

Kilbane and Jennifer enacted their pretend flirtation with vivid authenticity which caused the dowager to purse her lips and Mrs. Thomas to blink uncomfortably at the vicar, but

Pontley sat through the whole in the most negligently relaxed way calculated to raise Phoebe's spleen. The viscount was the first to laugh at the appropriate places, and the first to congratulate the actors when they concluded their efforts. He was especially kind to Jennifer and appeared impressed with her abilities; there was no reserve in his manner whatsoever, Phoebe thought disgustedly.

This attitude seemed to calm the vicar, who decided that perhaps he had read too much into the scene at the dining table. Since he had no way of knowing that his wife was only waiting for a chance to speak with him alone, he regained his usual spirits and requested that Glenna honor them with a piece or two on the harp. The vicar and Pontley were the only ones to really benefit from this performance, for all the others were preoccupied with their own thoughts and anxieties. When Glenna ceased playing, the dowager rose and announced that her party must be leaving.

Very shortly after this exodus Mrs. Thomas indicated to the vicar that she wished to speak with him in the library. They were gone only a short time when the vicar returned to summon Kilbane to his sanctum, and Mrs. Thomas announced that she was retiring early to bed. Phoebe and Glenna shared a commiserating glance but sat silent when they were alone to await Kilbane's reappearance.

The vicar's library was a comfortable room which smelled of leather and possessed several snug chairs as well as innumerable books, untidily stacked papers and an assortment of family mementos. When they were seated he addressed Kilbane haltingly. "I feel it is my duty . . . that is, when you are in my home . . . The fact of the matter is, my boy, that I have a great affection for you, as though you were my own son. It has been years, I know, since I was your mentor, but I cannot so lightly thrust aside the obligations I undertook then. When you stayed in my home I undertook your moral as well as your intellectual guidance." He paused to clear his throat and peer near-sightedly at Kilbane. "It has been called to my attention . . . well, I noticed it, too, of course . . . You did not behave as you ought at dinner," he finally said bluntly.

"You refer to Miss Stafford, I collect, sir," Kilbane murmured stiffly.

"Yes, naturally I do," Mr. Thomas replied, slightly ruffled. "You were very particular in your attentions to her, and even if she were not engaged to be married, your behavior would not have been above reproach. I cannot in all conscience refrain from speaking. Not only is there the fact that I was honored with your father's friendship, but I am aware that you have no one now to provide you with the guidance so necessary at your age. You do not perhaps realize that your attentions must be an embarrassment to Miss Stafford in her situation, and her aunt put my wife to the blush over your conduct," he concluded sadly, as he wearily rubbed his eyes.

"I did not intend to cause Mrs. Thomas any discomfort, sir, and I appreciate the responsibility you feel toward me, but I have attained my majority recently and I have every intention of seeing to my own behavior. Not that I do not feel gratified by your concern, sir, for I most certainly do." Kilbane paused to run a finger between his neckcloth and his neck to ease the choking cravat. "Miss Stafford is not entirely comfortable living with her aunt and she is finding her fiancé . . . rather restrictive. Being a spirited young lady, she is in need of some more felicitous companionship, which I have endeavored to provide for her." He eyed the vicar with some bravado, but his hands twisted nervously in his lap. "I pride myself that I have managed to cheer her and keep her spirits up."

The vicar regarded him with sorrowful eyes. "You are deluding yourself, Kilbane. No doubt the young lady is enjoying her chance to be with all of you and act in the play, but she is not your responsibility. Lord Pontley will see to her happiness."

"But he doesn't make her happy!"

"She would not have become engaged to him if he did not. I saw no evidence of her holding him in anything but regard. You have convinced yourself that she needs your attentions because you . . . wish to shower them on her. That can only lead to disappointment for you, my boy. Try to understand that and put yourself at a distance from her." He could not feel that he was reaching the young man opposite him, with his stubbornly set face and mutinous eyes. "I should not like to disappoint Phoebe and Glenna by calling a halt to the play."

Kilbane started to his feet in agitation. "Sir, surely you would not! Everyone is looking forward to it, and what of the village school?"

"I cannot allow such a . . . flirtation to be conducted beneath my roof, Kilbane. If you cannot conduct yourself with propriety during the rehearsals, I see no alternative."

Undecided, Kilbane paced about the room, running his hand through his curly black hair, his blue eyes entirely devoid of their usual laughter. The vicar watched him patiently and made no further comment. Finally the young Irishman stopped before him and said formally, "Very well, sir. I will not be the cause of disappointment to Phoebe and Glenna, or Miss Stafford. Our rehearsals will be a model of propriety," he offered bitterly.

"Thank you, my lord." The vicar smiled gently at the distraught Kilbane. "You must come to accept the situation; I know it is not easy, but you will be grateful in the end."

With a stiff nod, Kilbane excused himself. He was tempted to walk straight out of the house and not return, but then he would never see Jennifer again and that he could not bear. Possibly there was justice in what the vicar said; maybe he had not been behaving as he ought. But Lord, how could one see that charming girl thwarted in her buoyant radiance without wanting to take a hand? Certainly he could not, and, he admitted to himself at last, he did not wish to. His fondest dream was to free her to be as lively and animated as she should naturally be, to protect her from the harsher realities of life, to be the one to offer her happiness. Kilbane could not see the rigid, heavy-handed Pontley as the man to possess such an exotic wild bird. Had not the viscount sat through the dinner smilingly unaware of any cause for concern? That kind of insensibility would be anathema to Jennifer! Herself the most sensitive of creatures, surely she needed someone sympathetic. . . . Someone like himself, he admitted miserably, before shrugging off his cares to rejoin Phoebe and Glenna in the drawing room, where he was received with concern, though no one spoke of Miss Stafford.

No mention was made of Kilbane during the drive back to Lockwood, either. Pontley was, unaccountably, extremely good humored—polite to the dowager, whose countenance indicated her belief that he was a fool, and teasing to Jennifer, who felt a certain satisfaction that he was oblivious to Lord Kilbane's attentions. She was delighted that he had no intention of scolding her for paying less attention to him than to her new acquaintance; and any scenes that were to be made were her province, in any case.

The dowager's restraint was not so strong, however, for the moment they were alone she began to berate her niece. "How dare you make such a fool of yourself? I would expect

Pontley to be oblivious; he has no graces to speak of and wouldn't see beyond his nose. But you can't fool me, my girl. Twisting an Irish peer about your thumb and flaunting him before your prospective husband . . . Vulgar, that's what it is! Have you no shame? No, I needn't ask, nor any conduct either. You put me in a most disagreeable position, Miss, and I will not have it. Do you think to rouse jealousy in Pontley? He's incapable of it, and certainly would not feel it toward a baby-faced Irishman!"

Jennifer stomped her foot in rage. "Lord Kilbane is the most handsome man I have ever met and not the least baby-faced. He has more wit in his little finger than Philip has in his whole body, and is always the most charming, accommodating gentleman. Philip could take a lesson from him, my dear aunt, for Kilbane knows how to please a lady with his attentions and perpetual liveliness. Why, Philip is about as animated as a toad!"

"You don't need a lively husband, Jennifer," the old woman said coldly. "The last thing on earth I would recommend for you would be an indulgent, besotted groom. Pontley will keep a rein on you, be sure of it."

Her remarks were not calculated to soothe the girl, who had been encouraged by Pontley's smiling easiness on the drive home. If he could accept her flirtations with such nonchalance, she foresaw a rosy future for them. Jennifer enjoyed nothing more than the homage of a handsome young man, and felt it her due. If the stuffy Pontley would not provide it, there were others who would, and he had no right to object. But what if he was trying to trap her? Tonight the soul of amiability, tomorrow he might forbid her to continue her daily excursions to the vicarage. Had he not been mild about her performance in Hyde Park and then turned around and brought them all back to Lockwood in the blink of an eye? Of course, that was partly her aunt's doing. No, he was not likely to be so cruel, she decided. And if he were, she would ignore him. Jennifer turned away from her aunt and started up the stairs. "Good night, aunt. I think we have nothing more to say on the subject."

The Dowager Lady Pontley had a great deal more to say on the subject, but she made no attempt to do so. Watching her niece quickly climb the steps to be as far away from her as possible, it occurred to her that the more she railed, the more her niece would act contrarily. The thought of spending the rest of her days within walking distance of this inflammable, unstable personality exhausted her. That the next Viscountess Pontley had so little to recommend her beyond her appearance made the dowager's blood run cold. She had, over many years, invested her energies entirely in Lockwood and the dignity of the Pontley peerage. To see it fall to the hands of her nephew was blow enough, without adding the disastrous young lady now disappearing down the first floor hall. Her hopes for this generation were lost by the death of both of her sons, but that she should have to contemplate the ruin of the next generation as well with her niece as mother to it . . . Her pride revolted.

SIXTEEN

The rehearsal the next day was not a joyous occasion. Phoebe and Glenna were aware that Kilbane was attempting to retrench, but in his effort to keep a distance from the girl he was unwontedly formal. Jennifer was at first confused by this change of face, hurt and sad. Her eyes were large and incredulous with the suspicion of moisture about them, her hands fluttered in nervous agitation and she kept sneaking looks at each of the other participants. Surely there could not have been such a turnabout in Kilbane's affections overnight; someone had spoken with him. She went through her part mechanically as she contemplated who was most likely to have been the culprit.

Phoebe treated her much as usual and Glenna with slightly more kindness than she previously had, in an unsuccessful attempt to distract the girl's attention. Jennifer suspected both and neither of them, but she was sure they must be laughing at her for this defection of Kilbane's. When he did not take her hand, as he always had before, during the flirtation scene, she grew rigid with anger. There was an astonished silence when she slapped him and slammed out of the room without a word. They heard her call loudly for her groom and watched, still stunned, as she mounted and rode off. Kilbane groaned and dashed from the room but Jennifer paid no heed when he called after her, and Phoebe and Glenna watched him start to run in the other direction.

"Oh, Lord, what now?" Phoebe cried.

"He's probably off for a horse to catch her up. Poor

175

Kilbane! He was trying so hard to act properly, but he rather overdid it."

"Don't tell me you can excuse the little spitfire for slapping him?" Phoebe asked incredulously.

Glenna shook her head sadly. "Of course not, but it must have been rather a jolt to her for him to be so cold today after his attentions of last evening. Remember Peter told us she is known to be highly strung, and Pontley told me her nerves were delicate."

"Hogwash! She's a spoiled, selfish vixen and someone should take her in hand. I would think Pontley was just the one, too, for he strikes me as standing for no nonsense, but men are so foolish when they fall in love."

"No more so than women, I dare say, Phoebe," Glenna retorted with a speaking glance.

Phoebe flushed and bent down to retrieve a sheet of the script she had dropped. "Well, I will not excuse Jennifer on that head, Glenna, for I cannot see how she could be in love with Kilbane. She has only just gotten herself engaged to Pontley. I doubt *any* woman is that scatterbrained, and we have been led to believe that it is a love match."

Despite the constriction in her throat, Glenna protested firmly, "Well, of course it is. Pontley doesn't have the address Kilbane does, however, and I fear the girl's head has been turned as much by Kilbane's easygoing nature as by his graces. I thought perhaps Pontley was attempting to duplicate that last night when he was so very *casual* in the face of their flirtation."

A puzzled frown wrinkled Phoebe's brow. "Do you think so? Certainly *I* have never seen him more at ease. I suppose he had no desire to cause a scene, as you said, and if he had glowered at her all the evening we might have had a display of temper from her such as we were shown this morning."

"I feel sure he knows her very well, Phoebe, and treats her as he thinks best. Has she not complained of his strictness with her? And yet we have also seen him indulge her in her whims, so he is attempting to keep some balance for her high spirits. I think he can be trusted to do what is right and necessary to hold her affection." Glenna suddenly wished very much to end the discussion and be alone for a while. "I think I should practice for a while, love, if you will excuse me."

Kilbane had lost precious minutes going to the livery stables for one of his horses, and Jennifer had not proceeded at a leisurely pace, so it was half an hour before he overtook her. She was almost to Lockwood by this time and at first would not heed his pleas to stop and hear him out, but shook her head mutely, the color still high in her cheeks.

"Please, Jennifer, you must understand how it is. I did not wish to be so formal with you; the vicar insisted on it."

She was startled into looking at him. "The vicar?"

"Yes, he rang a peal over me for my . . . behavior at dinner and said he would have to cancel the play if I did not act with more propriety." His eyes begged her to understand his dilemma. "I could not ruin all our work, could not bear to think of not seeing you each day."

Jennifer drew in the mare and cast a quick glance at the groom following them at a sufficient distance as not to overhear their conversation. Her eyes filled with tears which overflowed down her cheeks. "Oh, Kilbane, forgive me for slapping you. I thought—I thought you . . . were mocking me for my forwardness. I have never been one to hide my emotions very well."

"Don't cry!" he exclaimed, hastily bringing forth a handkerchief to hand to her. But she was not looking at him and he could not hand it to her, so he leaned over and dabbed at her wet cheeks, wrenched to the heart by her distress. "Don't ask my forgiveness, I beg you. It was my own clumsiness which caused you such pain. I should never have been so particular in my attentions to you, but . . . I could not help myself," he confessed sadly.

"You have been very kind to me and cheered me immeasurably," she protested, raising her eyes to his. "Philip treats me like a child, you know, and he *will* prose on about how I should behave. He's so old and stuffy."

Kilbane was shocked by her attitude toward her fiancé. "But, Jennifer, you are to marry him! Surely you are not being forced into this match."

Tears once again formed in her eyes. "He was so much nicer when first I met him. *Then* he did not seem so old and strict. Oh, Kilbane, it is so wretched not knowing what to do." The tears overflowed once more and she allowed him to dab at them, but she was aware that the groom could not possibly avoid seeing such an intimacy. Well, if Philip was not around to console her when she was in distress, it was his own fault.

In an attempt to be fair to Pontley, Kilbane said judiciously, "I should not think he is so very old, Jennifer. Assuredly not thirty. And navy men are given to a certain discipline which will no doubt soften in time. I cannot think anyone would have the heart to deny you the least addition to your happiness."

Jennifer smiled tremulously at him. "You are kind to think so, Kilbane, but I cannot expect Philip to be so tenderhearted. He is often cross with me when I interrupt his work or suggest an improvement in his household. Why, I should think he would be grateful to me!"

"He should be delighted with every moment he can be with you," Kilbane asserted, leaving unspoken, but not unimplied, that *he* certainly would be. Hesitantly, he added, "You must not rush into this marriage, Jennifer. I don't doubt that your aunt and your parents are pleased with it for its worldly merits, but it may be . . . that your disposition is not well-suited to Lord Pontley's."

"No, I am afraid it is not," she said sadly. "But there is little I can do, you see. The banns have been published and my parents will come here sometime soon. There is not to be even a large wedding with bridesmaids and guests. No one was concerned with my wishes on such an important occasion." A heartfelt sigh escaped her.

"You must not marry him unless you are sure it is what you wish," Kilbane said fiercely. "Yours should be a life of joy and not of drudgery. Jennifer, promise me you will not marry him until you are sure of your mind!"

"I—I cannot make such a promise, Kilbane." She raised her head proudly and smiled wistfully at him. "You must not be concerned for me. I shall manage."

"Manage!" He choked the word out as though it were poison, but he did not say more, as they were now being approached by two riders from the direction of Lockwood. One of them was Pontley; Kilbane was not familiar with the other.

Pontley was startled to find Jennifer headed back to Lockwood so early, and in the company of Lord Kilbane, but he gave no indication of this. "We were just riding to the vicarage and had thought to see you there, Jennifer. 'Morning, Lord Kilbane. May I introduce Captain Andrews to you both?"

The name meant nothing to either of them, but Jennifer smiled demurely and Kilbane shook hands with the captain, at the same time intent on explaining his presence to Pontley. "Miss Stafford was not feeling up to rehearsing this morning and I rode after her to see that she made it to her aunt's all right."

Since Jennifer enjoyed excellent health, Pontley did not have to stretch his imagination to picture that she had had one of her outbursts of temper. He had never had much hope that she would make it through all the rehearsals and the performance without one, but he sighed inwardly for the reaction of the others in the group. "Are you feeling more the thing, my dear?" He noticed, with something of a shock, that she had been crying.

"Yes, Philip, I am perfectly recovered now," she responded softly, her head bowed.

"Good. Shall we ride with you to your aunt's before we go to the vicarage?"

"Why would you go to the vicarage now that I am returned?" she asked crossly.

Pontley could not repress the amusement she caused him in thinking that she was the only object of attention at any and all times, but she did not observe the twitch of his lips as he said solemnly, "Captain Andrews is acquainted with Miss Thomas and Miss Forbes and has desired that I accompany him on his call."

"You could go another time."

"No, my dear. Captain Andrews cannot be here long and it is necessary that he visit the vicarage as soon as possible. Shall we ride with you first?"

Jennifer was infuriated by his obstinacy, by his lack of concern for her alleged indisposition and by his cheerfulness. With a toss of her head she declared haughtily, "Lord Kilbane will see me to my aunt's. There is no need for you to inconvenience yourself."

"As you wish, my dear. I will look in later, of course."

"Don't put yourself to the trouble," she snapped, and

kicked the mare into a trot without bidding the captain farewell.

Kilbane took his leave of them with some embarrassment and followed in her wake, only to be greeted by her stormy eyes and angry comments. "You see how it is with him! What does he care if I have not been well? Would he postpone a jaunt with his friend to see to my comfort? No, never! He does precisely what he wishes, and has not the least thought to me. I might be dying for all he knows."

"But you told him you were perfectly recovered, Jennifer," Kilbane protested, "and he offered to ride with you to your aunt's."

"He did not suggest that I ride with them to the vicarage!"

"I shouldn't think you would want to."

"Well, I don't, but what has that to say to anything? What if I *had* wished to go?" And then, just as suddenly as her storm had risen, it dispersed, but it did not leave her to her frequently sunny outlook on life. Instead, she looked desolated and lost, a child bewildered by forces it could not comprehend. "He tries to be good to me," she whispered, "but he doesn't understand. No one understands. Ride after them, Kilbane. The groom will see me to my aunt's."

A minute earlier he would have been more than happy to do so; her behavior had been a disconcerting revelation, and one which he would have spared himself had he been able. It would have been so much simpler to return to Cambridge with the dream untarnished, her gaiety an exquisite memory for him to cherish, tinged with the despair of hopelessness. It was the romantic ideal and just barely suitable to his ebullient personality. He could not, in all conscience, leave her here alone, and what was more, he did not wish to. The chord she had struck in him was not a superficial one after all.

"What is it no one understands, Jennifer?" he asked gently.

Her body shook with silent sobs and she made a gesture of despair. "I could not explain, and it would not matter if I could. You see, even if I try to be different, I cannot. There is a . . . fire always burning in me. I should care, I suppose, because Mama and Papa and my sister have always urged me to control myself. And now my aunt does the same. Poor Philip! He wanted no more than to help me, and see where it has got him. I can't change, Kilbane, and I have never cared before. But it doesn't matter that I care now, that it hurts to see you disgusted by me. I suppose it is because you are young and full of spirits, too. Never mind. It is better that you know."

"Do you . . . get in rages often?"

"Only when I cannot have my way," she said with an attempt at lightness.

"What sorts of things do you want to do that other people deny you?" he asked curiously.

"I like to dress as a page and ride about that way. Philip lets me when he accompanies me. He was even rather nice when I imitated the Young Roscius in Hyde Park, but he brought me back here when my aunt insisted. I cannot stand to be constrained! When I am at a party I want to do something that will shock them all—climb over the sofas or dance on the chairs." When Kilbane laughed she shook her head sadly. "No, they are not all so simple. Philip saw me strike my groom once, and I lied about it, too."

They had reached the stables and he handed her down without speaking. "Do you think they will still allow me to be in the play?" she asked hesitantly.

"Of course they will." Kilbane stood by her, trying to think of what to say, but she knew there was nothing he *could* say, so she touched his sleeve fondly and fled off across the lawn. Slowly he remounted his horse and set off for the vicarage.

★ ★ ★ ★ ★

When Jennifer had departed so abruptly from her fiancé and his friend, the captain watched Kilbane ride after her and turned thoughtfully to Pontley. "An attractive girl, Philip, but she seems a bit put out with you."

"She often is," Pontley returned ruefully. "It's nothing personal, you understand. I promise you I fare much better than her aunt."

"Bit of a handful? I was surprised you chose from the schoolroom. Frankly, Miss Forbes seemed much more to your taste; but then, you were merely a navy man when last we met. Viscounts choose from a headier crop, I gather."

Pontley had no desire to respond to this jibe, so he turned the conversation to the vicarage and the play the young people were rehearsing. Without any notice, Captain Andrews had arrived at Lockwood that morning to renew their acquaintance and ask that Pontley take him round to the vicarage. The captain did not wish to have a message sent ahead, as he was anxious to see Miss Thomas's reaction in person.

In accordance with this wish, Pontley gave only his own name and asked for Miss Thomas and Miss Forbes, who were found in the drawing room over their needlework. Before the advent of the visitors they had a few moments to discuss what they would say to Pontley on his fiancée's behavior if the subject proved to be the reason for his call, but every thought of such an insignificant occurrence dropped from Phoebe's mind when she saw their second visitor. She rose from her chair with a wondering expression on her face and automatically extended both her hands to him, which he took in a firm clasp. "I—how—we had no idea . . ." Phoebe stammered.

"Unfair of me, I know," Captain Andrews responded—with a grin, "but I could not resist the temptation. When I found you had deserted Manner Hall without a word to me . . ."

Phoebe's cheeks colored rosily, though she appeared unaware that he still held her hands. "But I could hardly presume you would be interested."

When the captain turned to Pontley with a "For God's sake, lose yourself" look, Glenna hurriedly expressed a desire to show him the garden. In the hall she firmly closed the door on her friend and asked to be excused for a moment, while she sought a wrap. She also took the opportunity to advise Mrs. Thomas that she had left her daughter with a most respectable man and that their conversation was of a private nature which it would be a pity to interrupt. A tender expression appeared on the older woman's face and she queried, "A Captain Andrews, I hope?"

"Yes, ma'am. I'm sure you will be introduced to him shortly." Glenna pressed her hand and smiled. "I am to take Lord Pontley walking in the garden."

"By all means, my dear. I will see that the vicar does not intrude inadvertently."

When they were outside, Pontley and Glenna once again explored the empty flower beds with their neat paths and arbors. He studied her softly glowing countenance and asked, "You knew of this?"

"It was April and May every time they met. I could not believe he would let her disappear."

"And you approve?"

She glanced up at him. "Why, certainly. I think him a fine man, and we became acquainted with him on your recommendation. Are you not pleased?"

"Yes, I like them both. Does Miss Thomas share in your desire for a husband who is away from home frequently?"

"No, of course not!" she retorted, stung. "She worries every time she knows he is at sea, and it will be hard on her to have him gone so much of the time."

"A very natural attitude, I dare say."

"For a woman who is attached to her husband!"

"Ah, yes, I can see that would make the difference." He handed her over the stile into the adjoining fields, but she would not meet his quizzical expression. Abruptly he changed the direction of their conversation. "It would seem Miss Stafford was . . . upset at your rehearsal this morning."

Glenna could detect no emotion in the statement, nor on his face, which was blandly good-natured. "You have seen her since she left?"

"Yes, briefly. Lord Kilbane was seeing her to her aunt's."

"He was concerned about her."

Pontley placed a restraining hand on her elbow. "What did she do?"

"Her nerves were a bit on edge this morning."

"What did she do?"

Glenna could think of no satisfactory answer and began to walk again, but Pontley refused to be shunted from his purpose. He strode beside her and offered some possibilities. "Did she rip the manuscript to shreds?" Glenna shook her head. "Did she stamp her feet and rail at you all?" Again a negative. "Did she destroy your props?"

By now Glenna had stopped walking and was regarding him with astonishment. "Does she do that sort of thing?" she asked curiously.

"Oh, yes, but I presume she took another tack today. Let me see. Did she strike someone?" There was a barely perceptible nod from his companion, and he sighed. "Kilbane, then, for I doubt even Miss Stafford would dare touch you or Miss Thomas."

"He . . . was not treating her as he was used to do, and I could not blame her for being upset."

"Come now, Miss Forbes. There is no need to justify her temper. Why was Kilbane acting differently toward her?"

Glenna made a nervous gesture and asked, "How should I know?"

"I feel sure you do, so please tell me. Or would you rather I went through another list of possibilities?"

"The vicar spoke to him," she said softly.

"I see, and was the vicar present when Miss Stafford lost her temper?"

"No, only Phoebe and I, and of course Kilbane."

"Of course. Well, I think she has disillusioned the poor devil." He gave a resigned shrug. "I regret the vicar spoke to him."

"Well, *you* certainly made no attempt to put a halt to their . . . flirtation," she muttered.

"I thought things were going on prosperously."

"I beg your pardon?" Glenna was confused by the turn the conversation had taken, and she glanced up to find him regarding her wryly.

"Never mind, my dear. There was never much hope. I should perhaps warn you that Miss Stafford is unlikely to make mention of the incident or ask your pardon."

"It is Kilbane to whom she should apologize."

"She may have done so." He stooped to pick up a stone and toss it accurately at a fence post. "Have you made any arrangement for leaving the vicarage?"

"We had a letter from my cousin Mary today; she's delighted we're presenting her play and plans to attend the performance. Having had a gentle nudge, she invited me to return with her to her home for a while. I suppose I shall."

"And beyond that?"

"I have made no plans." They were headed back now and he handed her over the stile again, pressing her hand as he did so.

"Something will turn up." He watched her nod dubiously and silently cursed Jennifer for ruining her chances of happiness with an Irish peer.

SEVENTEEN

When Glenna and Pontley emerged from the garden they found Kilbane approaching the house wearing a distracted air. Pontley could sympathize with him and greeted him cordially, thanking him for seeing Miss Stafford to her aunt's. The door to the drawing room was open when they approached and they found Phoebe alone there. She met Glenna's questioning look with a wide grin, saying, "He's with Papa now, and no doubt Mama is hovering."

"They cannot help but like him," Glenna assured her with a hug. "I am so happy for you."

Kilbane could see that there was no explanation forthcoming from the two young ladies, so he turned with a puzzled frown to Pontley, who provided a succinct statement. "Captain Andrews is a particular friend of Miss Thomas."

"Is he? I see!" Just as he was headed over to Phoebe, the vicar and his wife entered the room with Captain Andrews, who immediately went to her side.

"Quite an audience we have for our occasion," he murmured with a glance about the full room. "Your father and mother are agreeable, though your mother's spirits are a bit low to think of you going so far away."

"She'll become accustomed to the idea, and she is happy for me." Phoebe cast a despairing look around the room. "How can we talk in this gathering?"

"Miss Forbes seems to think the garden worth a visit. Perhaps you would show it to me," he suggested solemnly.

When Phoebe and the captain had escaped, Glenna spoke with Mrs. Thomas while the vicar found himself with Pontley and Kilbane, who appeared to him to be at ease with one another in spite of the previous evening's occurrences. Nonetheless he avoided any mention of Miss Stafford, instead circumspectly questioning Pontley on his acquaintance with Captain Andrews. "He tells me his home is not far from Manner Hall."

"Yes, I called on him there on my first visit to Manner and met his brother, who lives close by with his family. A charming house with a view to the water, as you would expect, not too large but comfortable. The brother and his wife have a fine family of spirited children who adore their uncle."

"Captain Andrews mentioned that you have known one another for a number of years."

"Since we first went to sea, but our ways parted some years ago. We've managed to meet now and again, and we correspond." Pontley glanced up as Glenna joined their group.

She was surprised by the warmth of his smile and for a moment forgot what she had intended to say, but the vicar blinked at her curiously and she was recalled. "There is a cold collation in the dining parlor, and Mrs. Thomas thought perhaps we would not wait for Phoebe and Captain Andrews, since they may be a while."

Kilbane, never one to miss a meal, on this occasion showed no alacrity and ate very little while they sat at table and made desultory conversation. The newly engaged pair joined them when they were nearly finished, but showed no disappointment in missing such a mundane and unnecessary occurrence. The glow which emanated from Phoebe and the air of satisfaction about Captain Andrews permeated the small assemblage when they returned to the drawing room, where Phoebe explained that the captain would return in a week with a special license. "There would have to be a much longer delay if we waited for the banns to be read, for James must return to Bristol in a few weeks and this way I may sail with him." She turned to her parents a bit hesitantly. "I know that is rather hurried, but it seems a pity for James to have to make an extra trip here. Will you marry us the day after the play, Papa?"

The glance that passed between the vicar and his wife was melancholy but understanding. "Certainly, my love," he finally replied. "There is no need to present the play if you think it will interfere with your preparations."

"Pooh! And miss the opportunity to show James my acting abilities? Never." Phoebe swung around to face Glenna. "You and Kilbane and Miss Stafford will not mind if I do not help with the scenery and props, will you?"

Her friend laughed. "You'd only be in the way. Tomorrow and Christmas we won't be rehearsing in any case, and the day after I shall see to the backdrop. Jennifer has already gathered together most of the props for the three of us and Kilbane can do it for his two roles. There will still be plenty of time to get you organized."

The Irishman had not been paying as much attention to the discussion as the others present, and sat seated with an absent frown on his face. When applied to for assent to their plans, he did not notice and Pontley intervened. "I will be happy to assist in whatever way I may. Where is the play to be presented?"

"In the school, so there will be sufficient seating," Phoebe said. "Boxing Day we will go there and see what is needed."

"We have sent announcements of our project to everyone imaginable and put posters in the village shops. There should be a good audience." Glenna smiled at Phoebe teasingly. "Of course, we will be sure to draw more people to see you and Captain Andrews the evening before your wedding."

Captain Andrews, who had been content to sit silent through these discussions, now commented laconically, "A regular raree show. I have a mind to offer my services as a singer of sea chanties, with Pontley's assistance."

"The musical entertainment is to be provided by Miss Forbes," Pontley retorted.

"Then we are assured of its excellence," Captain Andrews returned gallantly with a bow to Glenna. "I see you have brought your harp from Manner Hall."

The thought occurred to Glenna that she could not very well drag the harp off to her cousin's and, although she said nothing, Pontley immediately answered her as though she had remarked aloud on the problem. "If you do not wish to take your harp to Miss Stokes's, you might leave it at Lockwood. I'm sure no one would touch it there, and we have more space to store it than the vicar."

Glenna experienced a touch of alarm at his reading of her mind, but accepted his offer calmly enough. It would be very dangerous if he could so easily decipher her thoughts, for many of them she felt must at all costs be kept from him. She had only herself to blame that he had found himself another bride; if she had been conciliating when he came to her as the new viscount, it was unlikely that he would have cast a second glance at Miss Stafford, so honorable were his intentions. Probably she should be happy for him to have found someone to whom he could truly attach his affections, but she was not feeling particularly altruistic that day. Besides, there were so many qualities about Miss Stafford with which Glenna could not be altogether comfortable. She drew herself up sharply. Pontley had disclosed that he was aware of his fiancée's defects, if they were such, and obviously accepted them. Certainly she should do no less.

Captain Andrews and Pontley were taking their leave before Glenna was aware that they had risen, and she flushed at Pontley's amused eyes on her. She was not even aware until after they left that the party at the vicarage had been invited to dine at Lockwood that evening, since Captain Andrews had to leave in the morning. In spite of Mrs. Thomas's protests that the notice to his cook was too short, Pontley had overcome her objections with the calm assurance that his cook would be delighted to put more than two courses on the table for a change.

Thinking that Phoebe might desire a few moments to herself, Glenna did not follow when her friend announced that she was going to her room. Phoebe indignantly came back to grab Glenna's hand and tug her from the room, murmuring in answer to her protests, "Don't be a goose! What should I want more than to talk with you and hear you say over and over how lucky I am? Come now, tell me."

"I should not call it luck, Phoebe. How could he help but come and offer for you? I have been expecting him daily."

"Have you now? You never said so to me."

"I did not wish to see you puffed up in your own conceit, my love," Glenna retorted with a grin. "But I shall tell you that I am remarkably happy for you, and that Captain Andrews is fortunate to have won your hand."

They had reached the room they shared and Phoebe sat down at the dressing table. She toyed with the brush and comb, fingered the boxes and ruffles. "I want nothing more than to marry James, Glenna, but I am afraid I will be so lonely when he is away. There is no one I know there. What will I do?"

"You will make friends as you always do, love, and it is to be hoped that you will find your sister-in-law a good companion. And then there will be things to do around the house, and I should think you will read about shipping and such so that you will understand what Captain Andrews is talking about. Sometimes he will take you with him, too, which you will enjoy enormously. When there are children I dare say you will be busy enough," she concluded dryly.

"Glenna, what will I do if he is away when I am brought to bed?" Phoebe asked, suddenly panic-stricken.

"My dear girl, you don't suppose you will be without servants, do you? And no doubt your sister-in-law will be with you constantly at such a time." Phoebe did not appear completely satisfied with this argument and Glenna took her hand and squeezed it. "Very likely your mother will come to stay with you, and if not, you may always send for me, whether Captain Andrews is at home or not."

"Yes, of course. You are too patient with me, Glenna. It is just . . . the jitters, you know. Everything was decided so suddenly. Next week I will be torn from my parents, to live with a man I have known only a few months and seen but a few times."

Glenna studied her closely. "If you wish for more time to get to know him, I am sure he will accommodate you."

"No, no. If I could I would marry him today! But I don't know if he really knows me well enough. You see, I have never been cross around him or impatient. How will he react when he finds I am not always so . . . even-tempered?" she asked despairingly.

"I see what it is! You think he will stop loving you when he finds what a truly despicable person you are," Glenna managed to say over a gurgle of laughter.

Phoebe flashed her a fierce glare. "Oh, you can make light of it if you wish, but it is very true that I am not the paragon of virtue he thinks me. It would be most difficult to behave so—

so piously all the time. James must expect it of a vicar's daughter."

"He expects nothing of the sort, Phoebe, for he is hardly addlepated." When Phoebe made to protest further, Glenna held up a hand to fend off her retort. "I do understand what you mean, my dear, but it must ever be the case. Two people who are attracted will always be on their best behavior. Surely it is the same with Captain Andrews. You will learn to accommodate one another, though I can see that the first year of marriage must be something of a revelation. You would be amazed to hear Pontley . . ." She thought better of what she had begun to say and fell silent.

Her curiosity aroused, Phoebe plagued her to hear what Pontley had disclosed. "Surely you did not tell him of Jennifer's behavior today."

"He seemed to know that she had lost her temper, though she certainly would not have told him, now would she? When he began to rattle off a list of possible ways in which she might have misbehaved, I was stunned. Why, he was perfectly casual in suggesting that she might have destroyed our props or ripped up the manuscript. So you see, my dear, that a man in love is capable of accepting even the most erratic behavior, and you could not compare with Jennifer even if you put your mind to it."

"But her flirtation with Kilbane!" Phoebe protested, astonished at this revelation.

"Did not seem to bother him in the least," Glenna finished for her. She remembered the strangely flippant tone of his speech and felt confused once again. "Anyway, I trust you will find that Captain Andrews wishes to have you just as you are."

Phoebe sighed and smiled. "Actually, you know, I look forward to finding out what he is like when he's out of sorts.

Do you suppose he will walk out of the house in a huff or not speak to me? For all I know he may wake every morning like a bear, growling and truculent. Or he may be full of spirits and . . . Well, I am anxious to find out," she murmured, her face coloring.

"Indeed, I don't blame you." Glenna went to the wardrobe and began to sort through Phoebe's gowns. "You should look your best this evening. What do you say to the silver and blue silk? I think it is even more becoming to you than the apricot satin because it is cut so simply, but the apricot is delightful with your fair hair."

Jennifer had recovered her spirits by the time the party from the vicarage reached Lockwood, and Kilbane watched wonderingly as she acted as though nothing had ever happened to disrupt the rehearsal that morning. Since the vicar was one of the party he treated the girl carefully so that he might not be accused of undue attention to her. Jennifer responded to this treatment by being especially affectionate to Pontley, turning for his agreement when she spoke, and proprietorially discussing her plans for Lockwood. This was accepted in better grace by the viscount himself than by his aunt, who appeared in high dudgeon. Pontley had seated the dowager at the foot of the table with the vicar to her left, and Phoebe's father had hard work of it keeping her in conversation.

It fell to Glenna's lot to entertain Kilbane, whose distraction was very evident to her. "When do you return to Cambridge, Kilbane?"

He stared at her uncomprehendingly for a moment and then declared, "I should leave a day or two after the play. It really doesn't matter much, you know. If I did not return at all the world would lose no scholar."

"Very few men are there to become scholars, I should think, but surely you pick up some useful knowledge."

"Nothing that will help me on the Irish estate, Glenna. I have learned, however, to play a good game of whist and a first-rate hand at piquet, to say nothing of the most dashing way to tie a cravat. I should not mind in the least terminating my university career."

"Are you considering doing that?" she asked, concerned.

Kilbane picked idly at his fish and gave a dreary shrug. "No, I don't suppose so. I had not thought much about it, but I will be coming down soon in any case."

Glenna felt a definite annoyance with Jennifer Stafford at that moment. To see Kilbane, light-hearted, carefree Kilbane, in such a state of dejection made her wish to shake the beautiful, heartless chit who was just then feeding Pontley a bite of her roasted cheese, her eyes leveled challengingly on Kilbane rather than her fiancé. And Kilbane did not miss the gesture in spite of his conversation with Glenna; his eyes were miserable, though he attempted to keep a polite smile on his lips.

The buzz of conversation around the table, ever sporadic at this dinner party laden with undertones, ceased unexpectedly and Glenna found herself asking into the silence, "Will you return to Ireland when you come down?" She had no other reason to ask him than that she wished to distract his attention from Jennifer and cheer him if she could.

Every eye seemed suddenly to be on her and Kilbane. Even Phoebe, who was generally too intent on Captain Andrews to note the talk around the table, chanced to glance across at Glenna. Jennifer's eyes blazed, and in an effort to claim the attention of those present she piped saucily, "Well, of course he shall, Glenna. How else would his potatoes get planted?"

Kilbane ignored her and answered Glenna as though the girl had not spoken. "Yes, I plan to live on the estate, for I have been an absentee landlord too long. My father always objected to the landowners deserting their properties to fritter their time in England in wasteful and frivolous pursuits, and I have come to understand his reasoning." There was a wealth of insinuation in the remark, provoked by Jennifer's sarcasm, and he turned to regard her coldly. To his astonishment no more than Pontley's or Glenna's, tears sprang to her eyes and she hastily pushed back her chair and fled from the room.

When Kilbane made a move beside her, Glenna restrained him with a firm grip on his coat. "Please let her go. It will do her no harm to suffer for the pain she causes with her outbursts of temper," she whispered sharply to him. Although he sat rigidly through the rest of the meal and answered Glenna with absent politeness as she continued to ply him with mundane observations on the weather and the progress of the play, he made no further move to follow Jennifer.

Ostensibly unmoved, Pontley continued to chat with Mrs. Thomas and seemed unaware of the empty chair on his left. Toward the end of the meal he proposed a toast to the newly engaged couple, though his remark that he wished them a long life of health and happiness gave rise to speculations in each of his auditors that Pontley himself would be hard pressed to share the same fate with his future bride. The dowager, still pink with indignation at her niece for making such a scene, eventually rose to lead the ladies from the room.

In the Crimson Saloon they found Jennifer, her chin raised defiantly, but the signs of tears still upon her face. The dowager pointedly ignored her, and though her exasperation was still high, Glenna could not leave Pontley's fiancée to her own shame. She approached the girl and asked softly,

"Would you come with me to refresh myself?"

Jennifer nodded like a solemn child undertaking an adult duty and led her companion from the room to a retiring room beyond the stairs where a basin of water awaited with cloths and towels. Although the water was cool, Glenna dipped a cloth in it. "Let me rid you of your tear stains," she said gently, and Jennifer obediently allowed her to remove the traces of distress from her face and tuck the wisps of golden hair into place. "There, you look much better. Did Lord Pontley mention that we will not be rehearsing for the next two days?"

"Yes. Is—is it all right for me to continue in the play?"

"We are counting on you, Jennifer. There is a good deal to be done before the performance and Phoebe will have other concerns much of the time. Have you gathered together most of the props?"

"All of them, I think. I have found the most adorable bonnet for me and a truly remarkable wig for you to wear. You would not believe the collection of costumes in the attic here!" Jennifer enthusiastically detailed her find as they returned to the saloon, meeting the gentlemen at the door. Her stolen glimpse of Kilbane showed him watching her warily but with concern, and Glenna gave her an encouraging smile. So Jennifer, her own eyes penitent, met his, and said, "Forgive me if I was rude, Lord Kilbane."

The Irishman smiled at her and took her hand. "I am perhaps too sensitive about my homeland, Jennifer. Let us forget the matter." He led her into the room as though no contretemps had occurred during the meal, and the vicar watched, half-relieved, half-anxious. He could not be comfortable with the tender warmth of Kilbane's smile at the girl, though he was pleased that there should be no more hostility between the two of them.

198

Captain Andrews regarded Pontley quizzically, but was only rewarded with a shrug and a grin, which Glenna could not help but see. She flushed guiltily when Pontley murmured to her, "You are too good to take Jennifer in hand and point her in the right direction."

"I—I did not mean to . . . That is, I thought only to raise her spirits, sir, and end any discord at your dinner party."

"Yes, and I am grateful to you."

There was no reading his enigmatic expression, and surely the light in his eyes was only the result of his partaking of a good glass of brandy, but Glenna hastily excused herself to seek Mrs. Thomas's company. It seemed a great deal safer than the viscount's.

EIGHTEEN

The days before the performance were filled with activities related to that event as well as to Phoebe's wedding. Captain Andrews had left to make arrangements with his man of business in London and to obtain a special license, but he promised to return in time to see the play given. There were no more expressions of doubt on Phoebe's part; she went about only partially involved in the activities around her, a delightful smile playing perpetually on her lips.

Her head full of props and Christmas, wedding preparations and thoughts on leaving the vicarage, Glenna pushed aside any sadness of her own. She noted that there was no more wild flirtation between Jennifer and Kilbane, but their easy camaraderie was based on a deeper level of affection which made Glenna even more upset. No one could fault Kilbane for his treatment of the girl, and yet the current which ran between them seemed far more hazardous to Glenna than the showy flirtation had ever been.

As he had promised, Pontley came to their assistance in preparing for the play. The Lockwood footmen transported furniture and props to the schoolroom and the viscount himself assisted Glenna in the painting of a backdrop for the country house scene. She was fascinated by his abilities with water colors; the two scenes took shape beneath his large masculine hands as though he were composing a melody which ran through his head. The drawing-room background she had started before his arrival was adequate, with its view of a large gilded looking-glass above a Grecian-ornamented fireplace, wall sconces and panels with the rough outlines of make-believe paintings on the walls and glass doors to the outside. But when he asked her permission to fill in the paintings, he drew a truly remarkable seascape and a ludicrous family portrait which Phoebe could not help giggling over. Beyond the glass doors he painted a country scene of lawns and woodlands, touched with humor by an odd assortment of dogs and trysting servants.

The outdoor scene was an arbor in the garden, and Pontley's eye for color made it come to life with primroses and honeysuckle, lilacs and laburnum. In the distance he painted a deer park, where one deer had a red ribbon round his neck. "A concession to your pet at Manner Hall," he teased Glenna, who had desisted in her efforts to paint, in honor of his superior talents.

"I had no idea you could paint like this!" she exclaimed with an admiring wave at the two scenes.

"There are many things about me that you don't know, Miss Forbes." Although his tone was bantering and his eyes mocked her, he yet managed to convey an impression of seriousness to her.

"Yes, well, that is only natural, but to have so much talent! I mean, I ought to have known such a thing, surely."

"I cannot see why, as I do not paint much any more. When I was at sea it was a hobby of mine to while away the long hours." He cleaned the brushes as he spoke, carefully replacing them in their case—one of his own which he had brought with him.

Glenna watched him curiously. "Why don't you paint now? You must have ample time to do so. It would be a shocking waste to put your brushes away forever."

"I only enjoy it when I am at peace with myself. The discord I transmit to paper otherwise is not to my taste."

"But you seemed to enjoy yourself doing the backdrops. I think perhaps you have forgotten whatever . . . discord you may feel while you painted, and certainly the results must satisfy you."

Pontley surveyed the scenes with a practiced eye. "Yes, I am pleased with them. It is seldom, though, that I have such an admiring audience and such agreeable company to temporarily achieve the necessary peace."

Since Jennifer's few comments on the work in progress could hardly constitute an admiring audience, and since she had provided no assistance at all during the project, Glenna could only assume that he meant herself, and she could find no response to make. She turned away from him in confusion.

Realizing that he had discomposed her, Pontley took himself to task. It was grossly unfair for him to either taunt or compliment her in his inflexible position. In an attempt to take away any heavier overtones to his remarks, he commented casually, "I think your skill on the harp gives you a greater appreciation of those arts in which you are not as proficient. Not that I count myself so talented as you, or as any other dabbler who doesn't botch it altogether," he assured her. Then with a lopsided grin, he added, "But I am not particularly modest, either, as you see."

Glenna could not but laugh at his honesty. "Oh, I could tell right off that you were not." Her face drew up in the charming, puzzled expression which made him long to take her in his arms. "It seems unfair sometimes that I should play the harp well. Do you know, I think of it as a gift rather than an accomplishment. Not that I have not worked at it, you understand, but many work equally hard for far less results."

They were joined by the rest of the cast then and Phoebe

immediately spotted the deer. "I think he has forgiven us for littering up the stable, Glenna." She turned enthusiastically to Pontley. "Your scenery is going to outshine our theatricals, I fear."

"Oh, no," Jennifer protested. "The scenes are very nice, but the audience will not see them so close as we can now, and their attention will surely be drawn by the players in their costumes."

Phoebe shook her head wonderingly at such want of tact but Pontley appeared amused and suitably deflated, his eyes dancing when he shared a glance with Glenna. "Oh, Lord," she murmured, "I have forgotten the time. Mary is due to arrive this afternoon."

"Do you suppose she will try to change anything so late in our preparations?" Jennifer asked anxiously.

"Mary?" Glenna asked, surprised. "I should not think she will even come by until tomorrow night when we present the play. The vicar should introduce her as the author, don't you think, Phoebe?"

"Yes, and I have not the least doubt it will go to her head. The promising new author of the year."

"Well, I doubt she has an ambitious bone in her body," Glenna retorted. "This must all seem rather a lark to her."

They had no idea until they saw her, an hour later, how much of a lark it was for Mary Stokes. She arrived in a truly regal fur-trimmed mantelet with matching muff and hat, every inch the celebrity. Kilbane had taken a room in the local inn rather than make Glenna give up her share of Phoebe's room to Mary, which was probably a good thing, since Mary brought with her an entire trunk of clothing for her three-day stay. Her delight at seeing them was unfeigned.

"Phoebe, dearest, your note arrived just before I left and I cannot tell you how happy I am for you. And Glenna love, I must tell you I am *aux anges* at having my play performed. Imagine! I have written to simply everyone in London to spread the word and I don't doubt that a few very special friends will even come down for the performance. There will be room for them, won't there?" she asked anxiously, her delicate features suddenly contorted with worry.

"I should think so," Phoebe responded dryly. "At the performance, at least. Whether there will be room at the inn is another matter."

"Oh, that's all right then. They won't mind stopping in the next town if necessary, I dare say. Martha," she said, turning to her maid, "do be sure to hang up my gowns straight away. They will be horribly crushed from the journey."

"I think we are to have a London opening," Phoebe whispered to Glenna as they climbed the stairs.

And the authoress was not content to merely sit on her laurels, but insisted on attending the dress rehearsal the next morning, much to her cousin's surprise. She did not upset the players, however, as everything from the acting to the costumes to the scenery thrilled her beyond measure. Jennifer was at first inclined to be truculent when she met Miss Stokes, but the first word of praise won her over. "Nothing could be more delightful," Mary rhapsodized at the conclusion of their performance. "Miss Stafford is perfect, absolutely perfect. Who would have believed you should have found such a diamond to star in *my* play?"

It was a relief to Phoebe to escape such gushing enthusiasm to return from the schoolhouse to await Captain Andrews's arrival. As the hours passed she became nervous, and finally terrified that he would not arrive. Glenna could not comfort her, although she could see that her friend was distracted and near to tears. In the end it was Pontley, coming to check that everything necessary had been done for the evening's performance, who took her in hand. Using the pretext of consulting her on the propriety of having the vicar marry him, rather than the cleric of the parish in which Lockwood was located, he bundled her out to the garden and walked and talked with her for over an hour.

His matter-of-fact acceptance that Captain Andrews would soon arrive braced Phoebe, and his admiration of the captain as a sailor filled her with pride. When he spoke of the excitement of the sea, she more clearly understood its call for some men, its challenge and rewards. And he spoke, too, of the loneliness which crept over a man, the longing to have someone waiting for him to share his burdens and his joys at trip's end. Rarely had Phoebe felt so gratified as when he smiled at her and said, "James could not have chosen better in his life's partner, Miss Thomas. I know there will be times when you worry about him, but your naturally optimistic outlook will see you through, and will be a great comfort to you both."

Phoebe lifted her chin resolutely and returned his smile. "Thank you, Lord Pontley. I have every wish to make James happy."

He pressed her hand reassuringly. "I'm sure you will."

Although it was almost dinner time before Captain Andrews arrived, his carriage having suffered a broken splinter bar which required three hours to mend, Phoebe remained cheerfully calm. Her only disturbing thought was that she wished Glenna had had the sense to marry Pontley when she had the chance.

True to their word, several of Mary's London friends arrived for the performance, which was just as well, for otherwise she would have been the only one wearing London formal attire at the play. Pontley had exerted himself to bring the dowager, and Jennifer was in tearing spirits. The play went off without a hitch, and several of the London beaux were stunned with Miss Stafford and her acting abilities. She was unnaturally shy about their attentions afterwards, however, and stayed close to Kilbane for courage.

Mary Stokes received compliments with the gracious air she had displayed on being introduced by the vicar. Not a cloud dimmed her horizon, for the rather serious young man on whom she had her eye was duly impressed with her abilities and asked if he might call on her at her home late in January. Even the dowager presented a rather less formidable façade than usual. She did not appear at all distressed by Jennifer's obvious reliance on Kilbane rather than Pontley, she complimented Glenna on her playing, and she told the vicar she intended to make a private contribution to his school project. Phoebe quietly suggested to Glenna that Pontley must have slipped his aunt an extra glass at their meal, but she could not wait for a reply to her pert remark, as there were so many neighborhood people who wished to be introduced to Captain Andrews.

So the performance was a smashing success in every way, producing enough money to see the school through the rest of the year and providing the audience with an enjoyable time. The only discordant note to the entire evening was Jennifer's announcement that her father had written to say he and her mother would be at Lockwood within a fortnight. More than one heart grew heavy at the imminent wedding, and Jennifer's was not the least of them.

In their room Phoebe and Glenna talked long into the night since it would be some time before they met again. Mrs. Thomas came by early and Glenna, feeling that the older woman wished to speak alone with her daughter, visited with Mary Stokes for a while. But when Phoebe came to fetch her, she immediately returned to continue their discussion.

"Mama has been very frank with me just now about men and women, Glenna. I—I think I understood before, but not so well."

"Are you frightened?"

"A little," Phoebe admitted. "James has only kissed me a few times. Well, there has hardly been an opportunity, has there?"

"No, poor lamb, you have been surrounded by troops of people every time you met. Phoebe, my mother died when I was still rather young, and of course Papa said nothing to me, though I think he tried when I was engaged to Pontley. Would it . . . be difficult for you to explain a bit to me? I feel dreadfully ignorant."

Rather than embarrassment, it was relief that governed Phoebe's reply. "You would not mind? I really feel that I must talk about it with someone, but Mama—you know, well, she is talking about Papa, of course, and . . . Anyway, I had hoped that you might just listen to what she told me and tell me what you think." With such a topic for discussion, the candle burned late, but neither young woman was the least bit tired in the morning.

The wedding was arranged for ten o'clock in the morning so that the couple would have time to enjoy their wedding breakfast and still have several hours of daylight for their first day's journey. The vicar read the service with moving eloquence while Mrs. Thomas dabbed surreptitiously at her eyes and Phoebe smiled ecstatically at her bridegroom, who returned her smile with one of suitable gravity, though his eyes belied any undue solemnity on his part. The vicarage was too small to handle many guests, so it was a small wedding party that returned there for breakfast. Mary Stokes, Kilbane, Pontley, Jennifer and Glenna were the only guests beside the family, but the occasion was nonetheless a festive one. Jennifer proudly presented the couple with a music box, and Mary had a pair of silver candlesticks for them; Kilbane had chosen an antique pewter tankard and Glenna an ebonized wood pen tray inlaid in brass and tortoise shell.

The most surprising gift was Pontley's. "You will note that I have spared no expense," he laughed as he handed the wrapped package to Phoebe. Within she found two framed water colors; one of James Andrews on board ship and the other of herself with the deer at Manner Hall. They were not perfect likenesses, but he had somehow captured something essential in each of them, and Phoebe impulsively stood on tiptoe to bestow a kiss on his cheek. "Oh, thank you, Lord Pontley. We shall treasure them always."

Watching her friend's pleasure in the gift, Glenna felt a momentary pang of envy. How could she ever have thought Pontley callous and insensitive? Nothing he could have given the couple would have charmed them more than the two water colors, and that he had done them himself made them all the more valuable. Glenna ached to have one of her own to take away with her, to remember him by through all those years she would never see him again.

When it was time for Phoebe to leave, she clung to Glenna, whispering, "Best of friends, write to me often, and come to see me when you can. I have never been so happy, and the only thought that troubles me is that I leave you to less than equal joy."

Glenna produced an impudent grin and retorted, "Have a care, Mrs. Andrews! I am about to face a new challenge, and you know how exhilarating that is for me. All my wishes go with you, love, for years of happiness and contentment."

With a last quick hug Phoebe parted from Glenna to take her husband's hand, her face radiant and trusting as she looked up at him. They entered the carriage and were soon rolling down the road while Glenna bit her lip to hold back the tears which threatened. Mr. Thomas stood with his arm about his wife's shoulders as the carriage disappeared from sight.

Now, Glenna thought, comes the other parting. It really is too much to bear in one day. And there was no hope for a word alone; Mary stuck to her like glue. Although they were not leaving until the next morning, there was no reason for Pontley to return now that the play was past. Glenna stood almost frozen as she watched the couple from Lockwood begin to take leave of the vicar, and she knew a moment's exasperation when she heard Pontley invite Kilbane to stay at Lockwood for a few days' shooting, an offer which was gladly accepted. For God's sake, she thought, why must he be so sure of himself? Has he not eyes to see what has been going on around him this last week? No, Pontley thought Kilbane had been disillusioned by Jennifer's temper and had been lulled into deceiving himself by the lack of flirtation between the two younger people. Glenna felt like shaking him for playing so fast and loose with his own future peace of mind, and her eyes flashed with her vexation when he approached her.

"I will have a footman pick up your harp tomorrow, Miss Forbes, and bring it to Lockwood at the same time they remove the props from the schoolhouse. You need only send word where it is to be shipped and I will have it dispatched immediately." The corners of his mouth twitched at her lingering glare. "You are upset, and no wonder, when you have shared Miss Thomas's companionship for so many months. I have no doubt you will enjoy your stay with your cousin, though," he remarked pleasantly, with a smile in Mary's direction.

"Oh, yes," Mary volunteered. "Glenna is bringing her

mare, and while she rides I intend to start another play. So gratifying to have one's work appreciated."

"Indeed," Glenna said dryly. "Thank you for all your help with the play, Lord Pontley, and of course Jennifer's." She offered him her hand as she said, "I . . . give you both my best wishes."

Pontley shook her hand and held it a moment. "Thank you. And thank you for all your endeavors at Manner Hall. I have a tenant there now, did I tell you? Glover is pleased with the family, and they didn't even mind providing their own draperies."

Although she attempted to smile at his teasing, her lip trembled and for one awful moment she was afraid she was going to disgrace herself. But he still had her hand and his grip on it became almost painfully tight, so she steadied herself and murmured, "I am so glad. Good-bye, Lord Pontley. Please say what is proper to the dowager."

The amused light in his eyes was the last thing she saw before he turned away, and she was faced with Jennifer, whom it very nearly choked her to wish well. When they were gone she retired to the room she had shared with Phoebe, claiming a headache which would give her an hour's peace. No longer could she restrain the tears which had threatened to engulf her, and she lay on the bed for some time, sobbing and desolate. Never to see him again, to have the warmth in his eyes fill her with pleasure, to feel his hand press hers. What a fool she had been! If he was autocratic, he was also thoughtful and kind. Lucky Phoebe to have one of his water colors . . .

Glenna sat upright on the bed, a bemused expression on her face. The backdrop with its two scenes would merely be discarded now; why should she not take it? Well, the whole thing would be too bulky, of course, but she could cut out the seascape and the ludicrous portrait, perhaps part of the arbor and the deer park. They would not last forever, of course, but perhaps long enough to see her through this aching despair. And she would have something of his with her when she left, no matter where she went.

From her sewing box she extracted a pair of scissors and dropped them in her reticule before she stole from the house so that no one would see her. The walk to the schoolhouse was bitterly cold and she encountered no one. Even the empty room with its atmosphere of make-believe comforted her when she remembered the hours she had spent there working on the backdrop with Pontley.

Glenna had to stand on a chair to awkwardly lower the scene, but she worked quickly and neatly in removing the sections she wished to take with her. The gaping holes in the cloth alarmed her somehow, as though they were witness to her folly, so she crumpled the whole and stuffed it into a wastebasket used for a prop until it overflowed. No one would give any thought to discarding it with the trash. Tucking the precious pieces she had chosen under her arm, she left without a backward glance.

NINETEEN

Mrs. Stokes was as indolent as her brother, Glenna's father, had been industrious, and her daughter Mary took after her. Her son Stuart did not, however, and he was always willing to ride with Glenna at The Oaks. She found him good company, and would rather canter over the frozen ground, the wind whipping at her face and hair, than sit in the overheated parlor with Mary, who wished to have an audience for each line of the new play she was writing. There was too much time in the parlor for Glenna to think about her sadness, something which she attempted to push out of her mind during the days, if she was not able to do so at night. Then she would draw out the water colors and scold herself for her sentimentality in doing so.

Since neither Mrs. Stokes or her daughter was inclined to make the necessary visits to ailing tenants or injured farm-hands and their families, Glenna gladly took their place, and filled her days with these visits and reading, riding and writing letters to Phoebe or her old friends in Hastings. The time was coming when she must decide where to go and what to do, but she felt strangely lethargic about her future. Three weeks had passed since she left the vicarage, and without Phoebe there to send her word of the viscount's marriage she did not even know when it happened.

Riding one day with Stuart she was detailing her experiences at Manner Hall. "I enjoyed it, you know, having charge of the redecoration and the household. If I could do such a thing again, I would."

Stuart Stokes was a rather short, fair-haired young man of serious demeanor and mind. "You should marry, Glenna. Then you'd have a household to run and you could choose all the new draperies you wanted."

"Do you see me so frivolous as that, Stuart?" she chided him. "I never even got to choose draperies for Manner Hall. It was the fun of starting new projects to pay for the repairs that I enjoyed. Except keeping bees. That was disastrous." She regaled him with the episode, cherishing in her own mind the more private aspects.

He regarded her solemnly for a moment when she had finished. "Don't you want to marry, Glenna?"

She threw up a hand in despair. "Stuart, you aren't listening to me. We have not been talking about marriage but about housekeeping. Marriage has nothing to do with it."

"Yes, but if you marry you can be a housekeeper, can't you?" he asked practically.

"I suppose so," she sighed. "It seems hardly worth it, though. I mean, I could be paid to be a housekeeper. As a wife I would be giving my services free."

"You'd get an allowance."

"Ah, yes, an allowance, which would probably be my inheritance doled out to me over a period of years. What a charming thought!"

"So you don't want to marry."

"No, not like that." There was no use explaining to him. With the usual male mentality of his class he saw marriage as the only proper role for a woman. Probably he saw it as a woman's protection, too, rather than her captivity. And of course he would be right. Paradoxically, she would be more free in some ways if she were not a spinster.

"Then I have a suggestion," Stuart proclaimed seriously, recalling her attention.

"You do?"

"Yes. I would not suggest it if you were looking to be shackled, because he would hate such a person in his household."

"Who would hate it?"

"Richard Banfield. He's a distant cousin on my father's side. You have never met him, I dare say, but he's an M.P. and has his aunt living with him as his housekeeper-hostess, only she's become rather dotty these last two years. He can't very well turn her off, of course, as she has nowhere to go, but he needs someone capable of managing for him. He's in London a lot, of course, but he likes to entertain when he's at home and he has mentioned that he wants someone who could be a successful hostess. But he wants no one around who is looking to snare him into marriage."

"He sounds a delightful person," Glenna retorted.

"Well, I should not make him out as a misogynist, but his wife ran away with a fellow when they had only been married two years and he has not come around to wishing to repeat the experience. Divorced her, of course, but he remains very bitter."

"I cannot think I would like living in the same household with him." Glenna gazed meditatively at the coppice they were approaching as they rode, and changed her mind. "On the other hand, Stuart, you may have hit on the perfect thing. His aunt would provide an excellent chaperone, and as there is a connection with my family there could be no gabble about such an arrangement. Could I meet him?"

"Tell you what, Glenna, I'll write him and suggest it. If he's interested he can come over to interview you. How would that be?"

Four days later a gentleman in a drab driving coat with

several capes drove up to the house in an elegant curricle. Mary's attention was drawn by the noise of the arrival, and she peered eagerly out the window. Her London suitor was due any day, and who knew, he might come early in his eagerness. "It's only Banfield," she declared, disappointed. "I wonder why he should be calling."

"Stuart has arranged for me to meet him, with an eye to becoming his housekeeper and hostess," Glenna explained.

Mary was horrified. "Glenna, you wouldn't do such a thing! In the first place, you have no need to take such a position, and in the second, you have no idea what he's like. Why, he sneers at women, thinking them all like his wife. I didn't know him before he was married, but if he was like he is now I don't blame her for running away from him."

"Stuart seemed to think that he became embittered *because* of his wife, Mary. It can do no harm for me to meet him, surely. If being his housekeeper seems unappealing, I shan't take the job. In any case, he may not want me."

"I certainly hope not," her cousin sniffed as a servant came to ask Miss Forbes if she would join Mr. Stuart in the library. "Just don't be surprised when he looks at you like a beetle," Mary warned as a parting shot.

Mr. Banfield did indeed treat her to a rather lowering scrutiny when she presented herself, but she met his gaze frankly and took the opportunity to get a clear impression of him as well. Of middle height, with black hair graying at the temples, he appeared to be between thirty-five and forty, with rather sharp features and thick brows that grew almost straight across in a perpetual scowl. His eyes were alarmingly black and unreadable, his lips pressed into a thin line. He was dressed in casual country attire, well tailored, and wore topboots.

His cold survey over, he turned to Stuart after nodding to

her and remarked bluntly, "I thought she said she was twenty-six."

"She is," he protested, turning to Glenna for confirmation.

"Yes, I am. Is that pertinent?"

"You look younger, which can only be a disadvantage, Miss Forbes. Please sit down." When she had done so, he remained standing. "Have you any experience in being a housekeeper-hostess?"

"I managed my father's home for many years, Mr. Banfield, in both capacities. More recently I spent several months at Manner Hall in Somerset overseeing the renovation of the house for Viscount Pontley."

"What made you leave that position?"

"The work was finished and the house in condition to receive a tenant. I am sure Lord Pontley would provide me with a letter of recommendation."

Stuart thought she was not puffing herself off well enough and added his own contribution. "Glenna did a great deal more than oversee the renovations there, Richard. She instigated several projects to produce income to cover the expenses of the repairs and decorating. I should think she turned the estate right around from a dilapidated ruin to a rentable property single-handed."

"Hardly single-handed," Glenna protested, "but I was proud of what I accomplished."

Banfield did not have a high opinion of what any woman could accomplish except to bring about chaos and disaster, and his expression clearly said so. His hard black eyes raked her open face and he muttered, "Indeed. Why do you want a position as a housekeeper, Miss Forbes?"

Glenna considered the question and her answer carefully. "I wish to have something useful to do, and I find I have a taste for managing a household. Then, too, I would prefer to be in the country than in town. I have a mare of my own and I have come to enjoy riding. Is your home in the country? Would you expect me to be in London when you were there?"

It was obvious that Banfield did not like to be questioned, but he answered her questions coolly. "I have an estate the size of The Oaks some twenty miles from here and when I go to London I stay in simple lodgings. No one from my household accompanies me except my valet. Any other staff I require is hired there."

"I see. And what would my duties be in your household, sir?"

"When I am in residence I have frequent dinner parties for which I need a hostess. My aunt is no longer able to undertake that responsibility, nor the running of the household. There are tenants to be visited, projects such as the village school and various committees to be managed, occasionally constituents to be seen, though I have a man in the nearest town who handles the majority of them. Some with complaints come directly to the house rather than to his office, however, and it is my policy to turn no one away without a hearing. I take my responsibilities as a member of Parliament seriously, and I need no young chit ruining things for me."

"I cannot think I would, you know. Dealing with people is a source of pleasure to me and I have always been considered level-headed. Do you stand as a Tory or a Whig?"

"A Tory, of course."

Glenna tapped a finger on the chair arm thoughtfully. "And are you an admirer of Mr. Pitt?"

"I think him the greatest statesman for the last century. Have you some objection to him?" he asked sarcastically.

"No more than any other politician at such a time. It is so

easy to shut one's eyes to what is going on at home when there is a war abroad."

"That war may be brought to your doorstep, Miss Forbes, and would be if Pitt were not such a tower of strength."

"And yet he promised not to return to the government when he resigned several years ago."

"He was needed by his country." Banfield flashed her a look of dislike. "I do not intend to discuss politics with you. It would not be necessary for you to have any opinions in order to handle any constituents you might meet; in fact, I would prefer that you did not."

"I can see that," she retorted, but with a grin to offset the sting of her words. "What salary did you have in mind?"

Stuart was aghast to hear Glenna ask such a question, but Banfield for the first time regarded her with approval. "My aunt has had fifty pounds a year and a clothing allowance for the entertaining."

"I would prefer to have a considerably higher wage and no clothing allowance."

"How high a wage?"

"A hundred pounds, to be reviewed in six months' time. If at that time my work was found satisfactory, I should wish it increased to one hundred twenty pounds."

"My aunt's clothing allowance has come to only twenty-five pounds a year."

"How old is your aunt?"

"Sixty-seven." Banfield eyed her warily.

"I doubt twenty-five pounds would go so far for a younger woman, and I presume you would wish me to look present-able." Glenna regarded him calmly and pointed out, "This way you would not need concern yourself with whether the allowance was wisely spent, or with an allowance at all. I would prefer that you have no idea how much I spent."

"And what if I were not satisfied with your appearance?" he quibbled.

"The same could happen if I had an allowance. You have only to mention the matter to me and I will endeavor to correct it."

"I am willing to pay you ninety pounds and no allowance," he pronounced flatly.

"Then we need discuss the matter no further," Glenna responded, and rose.

"Come, come, Miss Forbes. It is a handsome salary for a relatively undemanding position. You are housed, fed, and provided with transportation. There is plenty of time for you to ride and visit in the neighborhood."

Glenna was intrigued with the position, if not with the man, but she could not let him browbeat her from the start. "Ninety-five pounds and a review in three months to one hundred fifteen." Poor Stuart was by now overcome with embarrassment for his cousin, and she was aware of it, but she knew that Mr. Banfield was not the least disturbed.

"Very well, Miss Forbes. It would be wise, I think, to trade on the connection between our families, so with your permission I will call you Cousin Glenna."

"Cousin Forbes would be better, perhaps. Then I might call you Cousin Banfield rather than Cousin Richard, which sounds altogether too familiar."

"As you wish. Is there any impediment to your starting immediately?"

"No, none. I have imposed on my cousins long enough and can come when you wish."

"Monday, then. I will send a carriage for you." He nodded dismissal but Glenna had one more question, and he raised this thick brows as she stood her ground.

"I play the harp, Cousin Banfield, and I have left it behind to be shipped to me when I am settled. You have no objection, I trust, to my having it delivered to your home."

"None. I hope you play it well."

Stuart could not refrain from exclaiming, "She is accounted an expert on it, Richard! You will have nothing to complain of, I promise you."

The Oaks
26 January 1805

My dear Lord Pontley: I am to take up residence on the 29th at Grinston Manor near Grinston in Berkshire as housekeeper and hostess to a family connection, Mr. Richard Banfield, M.P. I would appreciate your sending the harp there. My regards to Jennifer and the dowager.

Yours, etc.,
Glenna Forbes

TWENTY

Kilbane moved into Lockwood the day Glenna left with Mary Stokes. Although he felt somewhat guilty in accepting the invitation, he felt almost powerless to refuse. This would give him an opportunity to see Jennifer every day until he must return to Cambridge, and if he returned to the vicarage he would not see her at all. Owing to his deference for the vicar, he allowed that gentleman to try to dissuade him from such a venture, but in the end he said only, "I appreciate your feelings, sir, but Lord Pontley has offered me a few days' shooting, which will be very welcome."

And each morning they did indeed take their firearms and usually had admirable success, the results often served at table later in the day. In the afternoon, however, Kilbane and Pontley usually went riding with Jennifer, who arrived one day at the stable in her page outfit, eyes defiant and chin lifted. Pontley said nothing, and Kilbane was left speechless for a moment. The scarlet livery became her boyish figure, and had a ruff to frame her stubborn face. She set her horse to the gallop immediately and Kilbane rode after her, while Pontley stopped to speak with the groom.

"So that's your page outfit," Kilbane commented when he caught up with her.

"Do you like it?" She was suddenly anxious to have him approve in spite of her earlier defiance.

"Excessively. Did you think Lord Pontley would order you to change?"

"Oh, I don't know. Generally he only allows me to wear it when we ride alone." She dropped her voice. "I wanted you to see it."

"There is no reason why you should not wear it with me. We are friends, are we not?"

"Yes. I have never had a friend like you before. Philip tries to be my friend, but he cannot accept me as I am. You . . . you know I am not *good* and it hurts you sometimes, but you don't try to change me."

"You told me you could not change, so it would be pointless to try, wouldn't it? Besides, what does it matter what other people think?" His face grew bleak. "But Lord Pontley loves you, Jennifer, or he would not have asked you to marry him. And you must love him or you would not have accepted."

"No! That's not the way it is at all."

Kilbane reached out a hand to tilt up the down-turned face. "How is it, Jennifer?"

"Oh, I can't tell you! You will hate me!"

"I could never hate you," he said helplessly. "Are your parents forcing you to marry him?"

Her voice was a bare thread of sound. "*I* am forcing him to marry me." She could not meet his eyes, but she knew by the swift intake of breath that she had shocked him, and she kicked her mare into movement. Pontley was approaching them now, and she rode over to him, her face pale and anguished.

"Do you feel all right, Jennifer?" he asked with concern.

"No, I think I shall go back to the house, Philip. Please, there is no need for you to accompany me. I'll be fine."

"As you wish, my dear. Send for me if I can do anything for you." Thoughtfully he watched her canter the mare across the meadow toward the stables, her body huddled forward over the mare's neck.

Kilbane's face, when he drew rein beside Pontley, was also pale. "Perhaps we should go with her."

"She wished to go alone. We can see that she makes it safely from here." They watched while she dismounted, a tiny figure in the distance, and then saw her walk swiftly to the dower house, which was much closer to the stables than the main house was. Satisfied, Pontley swung his horse's head about, but Kilbane continued to stare across at the closed door. "You don't look so well yourself, Kilbane. I had thought to show you Pennystone farm, but we can do that another day."

Without turning, Kilbane spoke. "She said she was forcing you to marry her."

"Did she? She exaggerates sometimes."

"I know, but I don't think she was this time." When Pontley did not reply, Kilbane moved to face him. "I cannot think what she means—unless you have . . . taken advantage of her."

Pontley took into consideration the young man's age and distress, but he had a strong desire to thrash him. "Set your mind at rest. I have not and haven't the slightest desire to take advantage of the child." His brown eyes flashed with annoyance.

"Forgive me if I implied such a thing," Kilbane gasped. "I didn't think what I was saying."

"Please do so in future. I am not a patient man and I have my hands full."

"Yes, of course. I—I will leave immediately. I cannot think how I came to say such a thing."

"Don't be a gudgeon. There is no need to leave. I assure you I enjoy your company when you have your head about you." Pontley rode on with Kilbane beside him, the latter too

223

miserable to pursue the subject further, and afraid where his tongue might lead him.

Pontley made sure that it was another two days before Kilbane had a chance to speak alone with Jennifer. The date of her parents' arrival was fast approaching, and he considered the more tension allowed her the better. It would not harm Kilbane, either, to imagine the wildest things before the simple truth was revealed to him, and as long as he made no attempt to return to university there was time enough. But Pontley was not indifferent to the point where uneasiness became suffering for the young people, and, after sticking to them like court plaster for two days, he suddenly excused himself on urgent business to leave them entirely alone in the library at Lockwood.

When the door closed behind him, Jennifer nervously plucked at the skirt of her walking dress and stared out the window. Gently, Kilbane placed his hands on her shoulders and turned her to face him. "Please tell me what you meant, Jennifer. How are you forcing Lord Pontley to marry you?"

Broken by shuddering sobs, her tale was all but incoherent for several minutes, and Kilbane rocked her in his arms until she was quieter. Then it all poured out: how Pontley had come and been attracted to her, how he had returned and continued to pay attention, but in a different manner. "He no longer wanted to marry me. But, Kilbane, I had started to depend on it. To get away from my sister and my parents. He was kind to me and he *had* thought of marrying me. I know he had. But when he saw me strike the groom . . . Oh, I don't blame him! I was so anxious that day; my sister was pestering me to attach him when he returned. Everyone just wanted to shuffle me around and have me out of their way. I wanted a home of my own!"

She gulped down a sob. "Don't you see, Kilbane? He was

kinder to me than anyone had ever been and I refused to believe that he was not still attracted to me. I know that is vain, but I felt quite desperate. My sister kept pinching at me to bring him to the sticking point, and she even urged my parents to stop at her home on the way north so that they might force him to offer for me. We didn't tell him they were coming and suddenly he had to go to his place in Somerset but he said he would be back. And he didn't come and they all pounced on me and . . ." Jennifer could not continue for the sobs which racked her.

"It's all right now, Jennifer. I am here and I will take care of you. Hush, my love. I understand."

"No, you can't understand! No one can. I was so angry with him for deserting me and leaving me at their mercy, forever harping about how foolish I was to think he would marry me. No one would ever marry me, my sister said. So I decided to prove they were wrong. I—I wrote to my aunt because I knew Philip was here, and I accused him of making promises to me which he had no intention of keeping. I cannot remember precisely what I wrote, but I said some very wicked things, and after all he had no choice but to marry me."

She lifted her chin stubbornly. "You may hate me if you will, Kilbane. I am sorry I did it, but that does not say I would not do it again. In fact, if my aunt were not so horrid and . . . and"—her voice dropped to a whisper—"if I had not met you, I would not be so very wretched here."

Kilbane shook his head unhappily. "But, Jennifer love, it is not fair to Lord Pontley. He has been kind to you and you have repaid him by trapping him into a marriage you know he does not desire." It was obvious to him that such an argument would not hold much weight with his self-centered child-woman. Even knowing that she was indeed unlikely to change, Kilbane could not resist his love for her. And she needed someone to love her—not the hard-won tolerance of her fiancé, but the deep understanding of a kindred spirit. Kilbane responded to the wild elfin charm and he was willing to accept the fact that together with the exotic heights of unfettered freedom, he would have to endure the depths of willful destruction. There was really no choice in the matter at all for him; if he could have her, he would take her, with all her problems, with all her delights.

"Never mind, my love. Let me take care of you, let me treasure you. I think we could be happy together, and that you would like Ireland. Say you will marry me and we can make everything right with Lord Pontley."

Jennifer bit her lips to keep them from trembling. "You wish to marry me when you know everything I have done?"

"Yes, Jennifer. I love you."

"And I love you, Kilbane. I didn't know that until I realized that I want to have you like me. It hasn't really mattered before. But even though I love you, I can't seem to behave as I ought. My aunt says I am unstable."

"To hell with your aunt! You need never set eyes on her again if you will marry me."

"She would be very pleased, I think," Jennifer giggled nervously.

"Good. Then she can plead our case with your parents. Will you marry me, Jennifer?"

"I should tell you that I am very expensive, Kilbane. Philip, I know, is worried that I will ruin him. I don't want to ruin you."

"You won't ruin me, Jennifer," he said with laughing exasperation. "I have enough for even so expensive a lady. Will you marry me?"

She swallowed a last little hiccup of a sob and nodded. "Oh, yes, please, Kilbane. And will you take me away from all my dreadful relations?"

"Just so long as you don't tell them they are dreadful, young lady. Oh, even then I would, my love, but I would be pleased if you would refrain from antagonizing them until I gain their consent."

"Yes, I see. I shan't mind living in Ireland, you know, and I will help you plant potatoes," she offered magnanimously.

Thoroughly provoked, Kilbane caught her to him and kissed her. "I don't actually plant my own potatoes," he confessed, "but never tell anyone."

They went together to seek out Pontley and found him with his agent in his study. Kilbane thought they should wait for a more propitious moment, but Jennifer wanted the matter settled and asked if they might speak alone with the viscount. The agent was willingly dismissed and they were asked to seat themselves. Jennifer did so, but Kilbane remained standing beside her chair.

"What can I do for you, my dear?" Pontley asked, torn between amusement and relief at the superbly solemn countenance she presented.

"If you please, Philip, I should like to marry Kilbane instead of you."

"And is Kilbane willing?" Pontley asked with gentle irony.

The Irishman flushed at the implication, though he knew it would not occur to Jennifer. "Yes, sir. Jennifer has explained to me the circumstances of your engagement, and I am hopeful that you will not consider my suit as an impudence."

"Not at all. I believe you are well enough acquainted with Jennifer to offer for her with your eyes open and that is the only basis on which I could object. Her parents are due in three days and you must raise the matter with them. I think you will find that the Dowager Lady Pontley will support you if you make an effort to gain her approval." He transferred his gaze to Jennifer. "I sincerely hope you will be happy, my dear."

"Thank you, Philip." With a shy glance at Kilbane she continued, "I am sorry if I caused you trouble."

Jennifer's temper did not always stay so meek during the wait for her parents, and they were several days late in arriving, but her behavior was no longer Pontley's concern, and Kilbane did appear to exercise a beneficial effect on her. Sir George and Lady Stafford, however, were nonplussed when they heard the new arrangement; apparently it was the last straw for them.

Taking them into her private parlor, the dowager made them see the light. She paid not the least attention to her sister-in-law's tears or threats to expire on the scene, nor to Sir George's repeated, "I won't have it." No solution could possibly have presented itself which was more satisfactory, to the dowager's mind. "The child is a spoiled brat, if not definitely unhinged. I tell you I have been hard put these last weeks not to see her to the door. Pontley doesn't want her and was forced into accepting her." She glared at them as though she had had nothing to do with this circumstance.

"Think of the advantages of her marrying Lord Kilbane— the chief of which is that he will take her off to Ireland where she can shame herself to her heart's content without our being any the wiser. If she is on our doorstep the scandal will be perpetual and mortifying. She's landed herself an Irish peer, well off to boot, who is well aware of her idiosyncrasies. Insofar as she is capable of loving anyone but herself, she loves him and makes at least a half-hearted effort to behave for him. Lord, you could not ask for more!"

"But it will seem so odd," groaned Lady Stafford. "She has been engaged for some time now to the viscount, and suddenly an announcement will appear that she has married someone else." She allowed her husband to wave the vinaigrette under her twitching nose.

"Stuff! It will only seem very romantic to the fools, and I doubt there is the least gossip to be made from it by the malicious, since we have all been stuck off here in the country. The only Londoners we have seen recently were at that idiotic play, and they will proclaim from the rooftops that they saw it coming, for she clung to Kilbane the whole of the evening and didn't even dimple for them," the dowager returned scornfully.

"Lord Kilbane might bring her to London," Sir George suggested.

"He might; he probably will one day, but under his influence you are not likely to see her dressed like a courtesan or imitating the Young Roscius in the park," she snapped.

"Did—did Jennifer do those things?" Lady Stafford asked faintly.

"She did, and we were only there a few days. I shudder to think what mischief she would have been up to had we stayed longer. Let her marry the Irishman, for God's sake, and be thankful someone wants her. The Irish are all half-mad and will think very little of her antics."

Sir George stood firm on only one point, and that was that the banns must be properly read. There would be no special license to suggest unseemly haste. The dowager stoically tolerated the overflowing household this imposed on her; Pontley's offer to house the Staffords was politely, and with horror, rejected by Sir George. Jennifer chafed under the wait, but Kilbane could only thank his lucky stars that the Staffords had agreed. It did not disturb him that he was abandoning his university career, which had begun to seem pointless in any case.

The most impatient party was Pontley himself, as he received Glenna's note long before the marriage took place. He felt it incumbent on himself to remain to see the couple properly married, so that there would be no cause for gossip on that score, but the brevity of the note and the information that she had taken a position with such a man alarmed him. Would not an M.P. be just the sort of party to provide her the kind of marriage she had originally sought with him? Frequently in London for months at a time, embroiled in a political scene which would distract him from his home life, Mr. Banfield seemed a likely candidate.

Only one detail provided solace to the viscount. When his servants had returned from the schoolhouse bearing the props from the play, the backdrop had been discarded against his express wishes. He had thought to have it kept in the schoolroom at the top of the house for future generations of Hobarts to use in their dramatics.

"I'm sorry, milord, but there were pieces cut from it. In that condition it could be of no use to anyone."

So Pontley had the harp shipped with instructions for the greatest care, and departed from Lockwood the day after the happy couple was pronounced man and wife.

TWENTY-ONE

Glenna was enjoying her duties at Grinston Manor, though it was trying at times to tolerate Cousin Banfield's annoying assumption that all women were fools or worse. His aunt was an ineffective but dear old lady who was so grateful to have Glenna relieve her of any responsibilities that she spent her days seeing solely to Glenna's comfort. The evening meal, usually attended by only the three of them, consisted largely of Cousin Banfield extolling the virtues of his party and finding some means to lay the country's problems at the feet of its female residents. Aunt Julia murmured consoling platitudes, and Glenna laughed at him. "I hope you do not give such speeches in the House."

Banfield glared at her. "You know nothing of such matters, Cousin Forbes. I speak only rarely in the House, but my speeches have been received with the proper appreciation."

"No, have they? I had no idea the members felt so strongly about the havoc females create."

"I do not express such views in the House, as you must well realize. There is a certain chivalry which must be maintained, even at the expense of a full disclosure of truth."

"Come now, Cousin Banfield. If you really adhered to such views you would be a menace to the country. It is the men who run things, so you may be sure it is they who get us into our muddles. Now if you were to give women some say in things . . ."

His face clearly betrayed that he thought she spoke heresy, and he refused to continue the conversation, maintaining an angry silence for the duration of the meal. But he had no fault to find with her management of the household, hard as he tried, and the entertainments she organized were beyond his limited expectations. Glenna enjoyed the company and made no secret of her delight in meeting her neighbors and conversing with them on their interests and concerns.

Banfield had never been able to put his guests at their ease, since they were couples—one half of which he scorned. But under Glenna's domain they were well fed, charmed by her open friendliness and, when the harp arrived, enchanted with her performance. The fact that the harp arrived without any note from Pontley cast her into a lowness of spirits which she had been able to keep at arm's length by involving herself with her new duties. Of course he would not have a chance to write at such a time, she chided herself. No doubt he was even away from Lockwood on his honeymoon and Mrs. Ruffing had been instructed to see to the shipment of the harp if a message came from her.

Assured that Cousin Forbes could see to her job competently, Banfield was at last preparing to leave for London, having already missed the opening of the session. There were several petitioners in the anteroom waiting to see him at this last opportunity when Pontley arrived at Grinston Manor. He handed his card to the butler before noticing the small group through the open door of the anteroom, and asked, "Have I come at an inconvenient time?"

"Oh, no, milord. Those are petitioners waiting to see Mr. Banfield, but I feel sure he will be pleased to see you first."

"No, I wish to see Miss Forbes. Would you just tell her it is a petitioner?"

"As you wish, milord."

When Glenna was informed of the caller she pushed back a stray hair from her forehead. "A petitioner who wishes to see me? But Cousin Banfield is still here, is he not?"

"Yes, ma'am."

"Oh, very well, show him in."

Her office was tidy and spartan but she had enlivened it by having the water colors framed and hung on the walls. Cousin Banfield had seen no point in providing her with comfortable furniture beyond her own chair and a spacious desk, but there were several straight-backed seats for her interviews with the household staff. She rose as the door opened to admit Pontley and suffered a violent wrench to her heart at the sight of him. Unable to speak, she stood and stared, dumbfounded, and then, panic-stricken, her eyes flew to the paintings which seemed suddenly to take on enormous proportions. Her face flooded with color.

His eyes followed hers and a slow grin spread over his face.

"I—I thought they were so good I could not bear to see the whole backdrop thrown away."

"I had intended it should be kept in the schoolroom at Lockwood for future theatricals."

Glenna covered her eyes with a shaking hand. "I had no idea, Lord Pontley. Forgive me. It was very thoughtless."

"Not at all," he assured her cheerfully, as he drew her hand from her stricken eyes. "I have brought you two of your own, however, so that you need not have such crude ones about you." He placed a paper-wrapped parcel on her desk.

She could not bear to look at it and turned away to the window, which overlooked the orangerie. "How do you come to be here? Is Jennifer with you?"

"No, she left with her husband for Ireland yesterday."

Shocked, Glenna swung around to him with her hands outstretched. "Oh, I am so sorry!"

"Yes, she'll lead Kilbane a merry dance, I fear, but you should not be too concerned for him. He is well acquainted with her flights of temper and fancy and loves her all the same."

"I feared it was so," Glenna sighed sadly, "but I meant I was sorry for you."

"Now, why should you be sorry for me? I told you once that I thought things were progressing nicely, but that was before Kilbane's disillusionment. Never dared I hope that he would continue to pursue her after that. You should congratulate me, Glenna."

"I—I don't understand. Are you saying you did not wish to marry her?" Glenna asked with patent disbelief.

"If I ever did, it was a very long time ago, my dear, and I soon thought better of such a fiasco."

"Then . . . why did you become engaged to her?" she asked faintly.

"Well, it would be most ungentlemanly of me to admit that she forced me into it, and you might jump to Kilbane's conclusion that I had taken advantage of her, so I will merely say that it was a misunderstanding." His lips twitched as the color rose once more in her cheeks. "Won't you open the parcel, Glenna?"

Relieved to have any excuse to avoid meeting his eyes, she obediently started to unwrap the package, but her hands were not completely under her control and he gently removed it from her and undid the string. "I had rather you saw this one first, in any case," he said bracingly, "so it is best if I present it to you myself." He placed before her a sketch of her in the drawing room at Manner Hall, seated beside her harp, with her face and hands swollen, her cheeks blotchy with color.

Silently a tear stole down her cheek, to be brushed away with annoyance. "That was not kind of you, Pontley," she choked.

"On the contrary, Glenna," he said gently, taking her

hands. "I could do no less than paint you the way you were on the day I realized I loved you."

"No, no," she protested. "You felt sorry for me, so mis-shapen and ugly."

"Did you think I kissed you because I pitied you, my love? I trust you have more sense than that."

"Well, I haven't," she retorted. "You certainly did not love me when we were engaged, and I can see no reason why I should think you did when you were about to become engaged to someone else."

"No, I suppose not," he sighed. "But then, you looked to be on the verge of accepting your Peter."

"And so you thought to throw me into confusion?" she asked sharply.

"No, Glenna, I kissed you because I had to, because I couldn't not do it." The same urge overcame him at her obvious confusion now, and he repeated his offense. This time she did not attempt to steel herself against responding; there was no strength left in her to fight her desire to do so. He cradled her against his shoulder and murmured, "I was so afraid I would not be able to extricate myself from Jennifer, and that I would lose you. Will you marry me, Glenna?"

The door was thrust open abruptly and Banfield strode into the room, a figure of righteous indignation, made doubly so by the posture of the couple before him. When Glenna made to release herself from his embrace, Pontley allowed her to do so, but kept a tight hold on her hand.

"So this is the way my housekeeper disports herself when my back is turned!" Banfield declared dramatically. "Charles told me you had a lord calling on you."

"Ah, but you would expect no less of a mere woman, would you, Cousin Banfield?" Glenna asked with an impudent grin. "May I introduce you to Viscount Pontley? We are just about to become engaged."

"Are we?" Pontley asked with a hopeful twinkle in his eye.

"Yes, well, you must see that I cannot lose face before my employer, Philip. I can do no less than accept your very kind offer."

"Then I must thank Mr. Banfield for his indelicate intrusion," Pontley asserted, and stepped forward to shake hands with the older man.

Banfield reluctantly acceded to this gesture, but growled at Glenna, "Your cousin said you had no intention of marrying."

"No, I didn't, and I had prepared myself for a lifetime as housekeeper to a worthy Member of Parliament. It is too bad of you, Philip, to upset Cousin Banfield's apple cart this way. Why, he had agreed to ninety-five pounds a year with a review in three months to one hundred fifteen."

"You wouldn't have gotten it," Banfield assured her.

"But then I would have left, and you would have had to face interviewing all sorts of wretched, incompetent women all over again." She smiled warmly at him. "Come, admit I have not done so poorly in my position."

Reluctantly he returned her smile, which he had never done before. "No, you have done very well and I shall be sorry to lose you. Would you consider interviewing for your successor?"

Glenna looked questioningly at Pontley. "The year is not over yet."

"No, but the dowager would hardly dare hold me to that promise now." To Banfield he said, "Let us discuss the matter for a moment, if you will."

"Certainly."

The door closed behind Banfield with discreet silence, and Glenna immediately spoke. "He is just about to leave for

London, Philip, and it would be very unkind of me to desert him."

Pontley studied her concerned expression. "Have you formed an attachment for him, Glenna?"

"For Banfield? Good heavens, no. Do you know, this is the first time he has ever even smiled at me or admitted that my work was satisfactory? Not that he has been unfair; he has never criticized me, either. But I did accept the position on the understanding that I would be here at least three months, you see, and I feel a certain responsibility not to leave him in the lurch."

"Men who have a dislike of women can be very easily attached when once they overcome their irrational prejudice. I think you would find that he would become dependent upon you, and he must often be away from home."

"Are you suggesting that I stay and try to snare him?" Glenna asked coldly.

"I am only saying that he offers you some advantages I cannot." He ran a hand distractedly through his hair. "I love you, Glenna, but I want you to be happy."

"And do you think I can be happy without you, Philip?" she asked, angry tears forming in her eyes.

"Oh, God, I hope not," he murmured as she allowed him to take her in his arms. "Will you need more than a month to find a replacement?"

"I should think two weeks would suffice."

"Enough time for the banns to be read. Do you wish to have Mr. Thomas marry us?"

"Yes, if you should not mind. Philip, if you think I am being unreasonable, too independent, over this matter of a replacement, I . . . I would do as you wish."

"Do you intend to be an obedient wife, then, Glenna? I could not believe it for a moment." He reached over to remove the second water color from the wrapping paper. It was a dramatic portrait of Glenna, seated on her mare, her red-gold curls tousled by the wind, her eyes full of enthusiasm, her face aglow with laughter. "That is how I see you, and how I always wish to see you."

Glenna indicated the paintings on the wall. "I thought I would never see you again, Philip, and I could not bear not to have something of yours with me. I felt so foolish to love you when I had once been engaged to you and—"

"Never mind, love. We could not know then how we would feel." He kissed her tenderly and pressed her to him. "I dare say I will paint you a thousand times and there will not be room enough in all Lockwood to hang them."

"Oh, dear," Glenna sighed. "I will have to transport the harp once more."

He laughed down at her. "At least this will be the last time."